I0565880

Praise for Hidden Truths

Clever, entertaining, and thought-provoking. On the one hand, Takacs explores the innate goodness of human beings, working together to solve common problems, reaching out to each other for support and comfort. On the other hand, the author replays the old battle between good and evil. In the end, all the pieces come together like a jig-saw puzzle of the good old U.S. of A.

JOYCE K. FAULKNER, AWARD-WINNING AUTHOR OF *IN THE SHADOW OF SURIBACHI*, *WINDSHIFT*, AND *VALA'S BED*

* * *

Action-packed and entertaining, it takes readers on a thrilling adventure involving corrupt, treacherous forces that will stop at nothing to prevent Christenson's leading-edge technology from being implemented.

SACRAMENTO SPECTRUM NEWSPAPER

* * *

A simple trip across the country turns into a life or death situation as large oil corporations from around the world plan to destroy not only the car, but the brilliant mind behind the invention.

KINDLE REVIEWER

* * *

How much disruption could an electric car, which not only generates enough power to run itself, but also enough to power a house, cause in today's run-by-oil world? And what will those profiting from gas-driven cars do to protect their power and money?

SAN FRANCISCO BOOK REVIEW

* * *

I was amazed at the twists and turns this book took, and not just on the expanded road trip. Futuristic in nature, but dealing with relevant issues, this is a good book for fictionalizing the problems in today's society. I recommend this book to anyone who believes...

AMAZON REVIEWER

HIDDEN TRUTHS

John R. Takacs

Red Engine Press
Pittsburgh, Pennsylvania

Copyright © 2017 John R.Takacs

Previously published as *The Take-Us,* Copyright © 2008 John Raymond Takacs

The Take-Us was awarded a gold medal from Military Writers Society of America in fiction and won Best First Book by Northern California Publishers and Authors.

All rights reserved. No part of this book may be reproduced or transmitted in any form or by any means, electronic or mechanical, including photocopying, recording or by any information storage, database or retrieval system, without the prior written permission from the publisher, except where permitted by law or by a reviewer who may quote brief passages in a review.

This is a work of fiction. Names, characters, businesses, places, events and incidents are either the products of the author's imagination or used in a fictitious manner. Any resemblance to actual persons, living or dead, or actual events is purely coincidental.

Paperback ISBN 978-1-943267-38-5
E-book ISBN: 978-1-943267-39-2
Library of Congress Control Number: 2017938437

Cover Design by Sandi Linhart
Editing by Betsy Beard

Printed in the United States.
Red Engine Press

My promise to you is now complete.
Rest gently in the arms of God.

Lisa Kristen Standen-Takacs
July 22, 1968 – October 14, 1994

Prologue

"Do you solemnly swear to tell the truth, the whole truth, and nothing but the truth, so help you God?"

"I do," Jesse said as he looked out at the mostly deserted courtroom. There were only five other people present: the judge, two lawyers, the lady typing, and a deputy sitting with his chair leaning up against the wall.

"Have a seat, Mr. Christenson." Judge Anderson said. "Tell the court in your own words what occurred on April 4, 1968.

"I was in the back seat when—"

"No from the beginning," Judge Anderson said, frowning. "And be precise."

"My two friends, Jim and—sorry—Jim Tassert and Dick Frances and I decided to skip school and go to Old Town in Chicago."

"Whose idea was that? Was it yours?"

"I don't think it was. I don't really know. We just kind of decided to go."

"Why did you three want to go there? Perhaps to smoke some marijuana?"

"No, sir...uh, Your Honor. I've never smoked in my whole life. We wanted to see what those hippies were like."

"Go on."

"We were driving down Lake Shore Boulevard. The cars around us started slowing down and then we also came to a stop. Then all of these black people came down the street yelling and were real angry. Some of them surrounded our car and were spitting on it and they started rocking it and talking about turning it over. We locked our doors and stayed real quiet until one other black guy—he seemed to be some kind of a leader—came along and told them to leave us alone."

"So that was the day Martin Luther King was murdered?'

"Yes, Your Honor. We didn't know anything about it, and really, I don't think I ever heard his name before that."

"So you left town after that?"

"As soon as the traffic started back up, we turned around and headed home."

"And then?"

"We were so scared we started slugging down beer...a lot."

"Where did the beer come from? You were all underage."

"Each of us swiped some cans from our dads."

"Are you sure you didn't supply all of the beer to your two friends? And then go on."

"No, Your Honor. They said my dad's beer was cheap stuff and didn't like it. I was in the back seat reaching for more beers and I looked up and saw the traffic was stopped. So I yelled out to Jim, who was driving, and for some reason he just plowed into the back of this stopped truck."

"The police report said that upon impact they were both thrown through the front windshield and killed. This was in a '60 Chevy? Those cars didn't come with seat belts. What happened to you, Mr. Christenson?"

"I was in the back seat and when I saw we were going to hit the truck, I threw myself flat on the floor and got knocked about and then got knocked out. When I came to, there were police and fireman all around."

Judge Anderson sat back and stared at the young man sitting in the chair beside him. "Mr. Christenson, you keep telling me you were just sitting in the back seat and had nothing to do with this accident. Yet you are charged with accessory to manslaughter. You just admitted to stealing beer from your dad. Underage drinking, truancy, and you were probably going to forge an excuse to cover it. Don't kid yourself. You did much more than sit in a back seat."

Jesse Christenson raised his eyes toward the judge's face and then quickly looked away. "I'm sorry, sir. I know I'm responsible for my best friends' deaths."

"Partly responsible, to be precise." After a lengthy pause while he leafed through a stack of papers, Judge Anderson let out a deep breath and spoke. "You will be turning eighteen in a few weeks. This happened while you were a juvenile, and let's see...yes, you are a straight-A student and a good athlete...and these papers show you have passed your physical and have taken the oath to join the Army. You plan on joining right after high school graduation?"

"Yes, sir. A little over a month from now."

"This is the deal your attorney and the district attorney came up with?" The judge looked out at the attorneys, each sitting at his respective table. They nodded in assent.

"Yes, Your Honor," Jesse Christenson replied

"Very well. I will go along with this. And because you are a juvenile, we will seal these records. However...look up here, Mr. Christenson."

Jesse looked up into the narrowed hard eyes of the judge.

"I have two more conditions. One, you will get an honorable discharge. Two, as you know the Vietnam War is going on, and I want your word that if they ship you somewhere else you will request a transfer to the war zone. Some might say I am being too lenient on you for these crimes. But truly, if you survive the war, a higher judge than I will have decided your guilt or innocence.

The judge slammed the gavel down, and the sound echoed throughout the cavernous courtroom.

Chapter 1

The Beginning

"Jump…jump!"

His arms were splayed out like Jesus on the cross. He stuck out his middle fingers, which were clearly visible all the way down to the street fourteen stories below—even with the heavy leather gloves on.

"Are you gonna jump or what?" Jimmie yelled across the forty-foot span of open air that separated them. They had been partners for a couple of years now, working high iron.

Jesse squinted in the bright sunshine, tasting the stench of the black diesel fumes drifting up. He turned to Jimmie, pointed his middle finger like a gun, and with his ring finger pulled the trigger. He was standing on top of an H-column in the financial district of San Francisco, trying to stretch a kink out of his back.

"Come on, if you jump I can go to the bar and toast you."

"Anything for a beer…I think you're still at war with the white man."

Jimmie was half Native American. His face had on that shit-eating grin he usually wore. He had little fear and was horrible to watch on the iron; his sense of balance was terrible. Jesse saw him a couple of times crawling back up onto a floor beam that he'd fallen off. If Jimmie hadn't caught the edge of the beam with his extra-long, powerful arms he would have gone in the hole. After a couple of stories up, going in the hole meant certain death.

"Jesse, watch your back," Jimmie yelled. "You got it?"

Jesse was still standing upright; the iron this afternoon was hot enough to fry an egg on. There were three beams, attached one below the other under the crane's "headache ball," swinging in behind his head. He looked down at the operator and put his thumb down, a signal to keep booming down. The operator, Gar, was a close friend. It paid to have a good friend in the crane cab. Your life was in his hands.

"Yeah, I got it," he yelled back over to Jimmie. Jimmie almost always took the "easy end" of the beam. Easy end wasn't that easy, but on the other hand, Jesse was always dangling in space.

The wind was up today and the iron was swinging like a helicopter blade. Jesse caught the beam, which weighed a couple of thousand pounds, and slowed it down, releasing it only when it started to pull him off the building. When the other end of the beam came slowly around, he slammed it into position, stuck one bolt in it, spun a nut on it, and jumped up onto the top flange and ran to the choker. The whole process took just seconds.

Jesse was the nimble one; "Catty" was what other ironworkers said when they referred to him.

"Can't you make your end, pussy?" he hollered to Jimmie.

"This iron is shit. We been fighting this crap all the way up," Jimmie said in his deep voice, never asking for help—which of course was the signal he needed it. Jimmie was the taller of the two by at least four inches. He was maybe six-five or -six. It was hard to tell because he never stood up straight, but he was as strong and sturdy as a grizzly bear.

Jesse walked over, pulled out his sleever bar, sat down on the hot iron, and caught a hole. He wasn't exactly a weakling. "Ready, on three. One...two...three." He pulled on the bar, muscles rippling. The beam started to move slowly and then unceremoniously snapped into place.

He stood up on the top flange of the beam, walked back, and removed the choker before setting the next two swaying beams. When finished, he went back over to the street side and looked down as he waited for the next pick. He loved this job. It was hard, fast, and dangerous. No one dared fuck with him, and he only had to talk to one or two people a day. The only problem was that it was date-certain, exactly like a pro quarterback's job. It wasn't a matter of if you were going to be hurt, but *when*. Jesse was thirty-nine-years old, and in his heart he knew his time was nearing.

When he got out of the Army, Jesse had enrolled in college like so many other vets. It was difficult, and he only lasted one year. It wasn't the schoolwork; that was a breeze. He was a pre-med major with a 4.0 GPA, but it was being around so many pimple-faced, idealistic kids. He was twenty-two at the time and was a steely-eyed killer. When the counselor called and asked why he wasn't coming back, Jesse told him truthfully that he really didn't like people that much. The only exceptions were the faceless young women he met everywhere. There was a sexual revolution going on, and he benefited from it big time.

The summer after his attempt at college, a high school friend told him the ironworkers were hiring, and they didn't care if you were a veteran or not. In the years following the war it was better to say you'd been hitchhiking around the country for three years than to tell a prospective employer you were a war vet. Back then he was part of the most despised and hated segment of the American population: white Vietnam vet—a.k.a. baby killer.

He applied for the ironworker job, and when he had his interview, the business agent asked, "Are you afraid of heights?"

"I used to be a paratrooper, sir."

The business agent shook his head. "We don't issue parachutes here. If you fall off a building, just remember not to scream on the way down. You're going to die anyway, no sense embarrassing yourself. And you don't have to call me 'sir.' We all work for a living here."

Jesse knew he had found a home. That was sixteen years ago.

"Jesse!" his pusher called out.

"What's up, Roger?" He looked down a floor.

"After this pick, come down. The eagle shit big time. This week we got our bonus from the early finish on the last building." The supervisor fanned his face with the crew's paychecks.

"Oh, man, that's going to give me a Dalai Lama."

"What's the dilemma?"

"Should I buy a new racing motorcycle or a new parachute?"

"You need to give up that dangerous shit." Roger pointed up, his shirt whipping in the breeze. "You better look up, there's your last piece."

"Dangerous? Nah, it's what I do to relax." Jesse reached up, caught the last piece of iron for the day, and began the process of putting it in place. These steel-framed buildings were nothing more than giant erector sets. When he was finished, he slid down the column to the next floor, where his supervisor was waiting.

"What are you doing this weekend?" Roger asked, handing him the check.

"I was going to go riding, but Gar has a real date. I think I'll get my rig and do some skydiving."

"You're not going out chasing wild women?"

"You said 'this weekend.' It's still Friday and I just got paid. What do you think I'm going to do? I do have an image to keep up."

"Yeah, right. Why don't you come over Saturday for a steak on the barbie? Brenda has a friend coming by she wants you to meet."

"Not one of those again." He held out his arms as if he were trying to hug a fifty-five-gallon barrel.

"I've met this one. She's your type."

Jimmie walked up to them and said, "What type? Eight to eighty, and deaf, dumb, or blind?"

"How come it took you so long to climb down? Did you fall off the building and have to take the elevator back up?" Jesse shot back.

"I know your type, Jesse boy," Jimmie said, ignoring the dig. "'When they're old enough to pee, they're old enough for me.'"

They all burst out laughing.

"Jesse, you know better than going after an Injun. They're still at war with us white men," Roger said. "Look, this girl's perfect—cute, built like a brick shithouse, and—"

"Let me guess, a bartender," Jesse said.

"Better. A nurse."

"Damn, Jesse," Jimmie said, suddenly reaching out and trying to snatch Jesse's check. "Think of how much money, not counting blood, you could save. You could be a zillionaire."

Jesse moved easily out of reach. "You're implying that I'm accident-prone?" He looked down at the dried blood on his arm.

"It's lucky you weren't around when my people were taking scalps. Your skin is so thin we would've had to invent a new type of knife, more like a scalpel." Jimmie laughed, fingering the buck knife he always carried. "You gonna go meet her or what?"

"After a threat like that, how can I say no?"

Chapter 2

The Idea

He saw her as soon as he walked in. She wasn't hard to miss with her waist-length brown hair, and she filled the spaghetti-strapped sun dress like a Hollywood starlet, as promised. She was talking to Roger's wife Brenda. Never being the shy one, Jesse walked right up and started to hit on her.

"Hi, I'm Jesse, your new fiancé."

She turned slowly to look at him, eyes wide, and then looked back at Brenda. "He is a handsome dickhead, isn't he?"

"Damn, bad first impression," Jesse said, snapping his fingers. "Brenda, could you make the proper introductions, please?"

"Kristin, this is Jesse Christenson. Dickhead, this is my good, probably-too-good-for-you, friend Kristin." Brenda put her arms around Jesse and gave him a small kiss. "I'm glad you have such a good sense of humor."

"I'm so crushed, I'm in need of fine spirits to revive me," he said, hand over his heart.

"I'll get you a beer," Brenda said, walking away.

"So, you're a nurse?" Jesse asked, looking down into Kristen's sizzling blue eyes.

"Yes, and I hear you're an accident waiting to happen."

"World's a dangerous place."

"It seems you have a way of making it more so. You have a very dangerous job and, I hear, a few high-impact hobbies—impact like when your body hits the ground."

"You certainly don't like to skirt around the edge of the pond, do you?"

"Look, you're the one who said you were my future fiancé. I don't want to end up a young widow." She laughed then and it sounded like angel wings to his ears. "You're uncomfortable and afraid with anybody who cares about you, aren't you?"

Jesse had been blessed with a great sense of balance, but right now he was starting to reel. This beautiful woman was getting too close to the truth. "You might not believe this, but I don't have a sense of fear. None."

"Then how come you've never been married?" She stood very close to him, looking straight up into his eyes. He could smell her luscious perfume. "No long-time girlfriend. I hear you're not gay. That tells me you're afraid of commitment. That is a listed fear, dear." With that, she reached up with her small fingers and gently touched the end of his nose.

"You wanna make out?" he asked, trying to steer the conversation in a different direction.

"I'm not an easy flop. But for a dinner date, who knows? Maybe you'll get lucky."

"Dinner, huh?"

"I see you two are getting along," Brenda said, handing him a beer.

He took a large gulp.

"He's already asked me out for dinner."

He nearly spit out his beer on the two of them. "I asked you to dinner?"

"See, he did it again, just in very poor English. But, okay, I accept." They both started laughing. "Next Friday is fine by me. And congratulations, you're already on the road to curing your fears."

***

Jesse watched the last of the oil drip into the sawed-off five gallon plastic bucket. He crawled out from under Kristin's Forerunner and looked up from the detached garage to the main house he had finished just six months before. It had been two years since he and Kristin had married. They were fortunate to have discovered fifty acres with a rambling creek running through the tall, wild forest.

Together they'd designed and built a unique, two-story cedar home with many bright, wide-open windows. He smiled. They did everything together. Kristen helped somewhat, but he'd done most of the work, all those rough years in construction finally paying off. He looked closely at the hand-built spire atop the roof and humbly admired his own workmanship. There was no doubt in his mind that there was a special dispensation granted to those who built their own homes.

As he sat on the dirt tossing small rocks, the last of the sun disappeared behind some ominous-looking clouds. He thought about all the compromises he'd had to make. No more motorcycle racing; instead he could street cruise. Absolutely no more skydiving; she thought a good alternative was to get his pilot's license. And he had to take one of the safer supervisory jobs that were constantly being offered to him. She was adamant about all of it, stating that if he wanted her, he would have to choose *life*. Never having fallen in love before, he knew not that small sacrifices were the norm. The wildness of his old life became a distant memory, especially with a woman like Kristin.

God, he was lucky to have found such an athletic, outdoorsy girl. She liked to hike in the summer and ski in the winter up in the Sierras. He, too, loved the mountains. They gave him a special release, almost a sense of rebirth. After all his subconscious attempts to kill himself for so many years, spring had forced its way back into his life, and he'd finally found the happiness that he thought was reserved for only "nice" people. He was at peace for the first time since Nam.

The sound of thunder growling in the distance, its echoes bouncing off the canyon walls, brought him out of his brief reverie. The weather at this altitude on the west slope of the Sierras was, for the most part, sunny and bright. But there were the inevitable, sudden storms that kicked up. Some would come fiercely howling, like the coyotes, right to their doorstep. He looked up at the sky and saw it was turning dark. This was going to be a furious storm. He hurriedly crawled back under the SUV.

"Honey, lunch is ready," Kristin called.

"Okay. Ouch! Oh, shit!" He hit his head on the exhaust pipe when he shifted his position, and a rock poked him between his shoulder blades.

"Hey, Jesse-boy, you're not getting much done under there, are you?" she asked, a sweet tone in her voice.

"What makes you think that?" He reached for a ratchet and socket to finish putting on the skid plate.

"Well, usually if I hear you shout 'fuck' or 'shit' or a combination like 'I'd like to get hold of the little Jap bastard that designed this muffler bearing—I'd rip his fucking head off and shit down his throat,' then I'd know you were truly getting something done. Are you bleeding yet?"

"Mufflers don't have bearings," he said, all he could manage while squirming out from under the SUV. "A fuck shit is good for a man to say once in a while. It's…therapeutic." He stood up and brushed the dirt off his jeans.

Kristen looked down at the top of his right hand, which was bleeding. "I think the only therapy you're going to need is a blood transfusion."

She had a point there. It seemed he could never work on anything without bleeding.

"It's just a small sacrifice to the God of Automobiles for allowing me to get something done," he said.

"Yeah, and if you keep talking like that, the God of the Universe is going to throw down some lightning and cauterize your whole body."

He smiled. Cauterize. Only she would use such a word.

"Honey," she said, taking his wounded hand in hers and peering closely at it as they walked back to the house. "What you said this morning. You really mean it?"

"That I adore you? You know me—I'll say anything for sex."

"No, not that. I know you rise up at the mere sight of me, especially naked."

He pointed to a large boulder with his bloody hand. "How about now? We could break that rock in."

"We already broke that rock in. Come on, I'm being serious," she said, twirling her long hair with her free hand as they walked.

"What *did* I say this morning?"

"What you said about your invention."

"The Autodog?"

She just looked at him with those big, open eyes. "Not that. And, oh, by the way, it got jammed today, and you need to clean up the big pile of dog food before Thor gets into it and eats it all."

His latest invention was a revolutionary, dog-food storage and dispensing system that hung on the wall and held up to fifty pounds of kibble. Empty that big bag of food into it, throw the bag away, and create more room in the pantry, a real necessity in a house like theirs. "It must be those weak springs I bought. What I really need is more money to properly engineer it," he said, seeing the problem in his mind's eye.

"I thought you said if we could sell Autodogs, we would have more money." A small smile touched her pretty lips.

"It just doesn't seem right. Every time I get a great idea, we're broke. Then all I can do is wish I could win the lotto so we could be rich, so we could make the Autodog to become rich. Did that... make any sense?"

"Just about normal for you. The only reason we're temporarily broke is that we took all our savings to pay cash for this place." She looked up, pulled him down, and gave him a great big, wet kiss. "You got it all wrong, though. We're in love, so we're already rich. What you want is wealth. And one day you will take us down that road, and it will happen. But I wasn't talking about the Autodog. I meant what you said about your dream, the car that uses no gasoline. Do you really think it would work? What would you call it?"

He put his arms around her and drew her close, mindful not

to touch her with his greasy, bloody hands. "After that speech, I'd call it the Take-Us. Like Take-Us down that road, or Take-Us to the bank. Or better yet, Take-Us away. It's such a simple idea. I can't understand why somebody hasn't already invented it."

"Your Autodog is a simple idea, and it isn't on the market yet, either."

Jesse looked down into Kristen's eyes. He felt so much love he actually thought his heart would burst clean out of his chest. "All things have their time," he said as his stomach chose that moment to let out a growl.

"Like time to eat." She rubbed his flat, hard stomach.

"How about I have you for lunch?"

She wiggled away. "How about you can have me for a midnight snack. I have to take Thor down to the vet and then go to the city for groceries. After that, I'm meeting Laura and a couple of friends for a drink."

"No drunk driving, right?"

"I'm a nurse and I'm going to have our baby. What do you think?"

"That you're going to make a great mother."

After lunch, she kissed him goodbye and he went back to work, this time on his Ford pickup. The sound of thunder reverberated around him. It was getting closer, and the first fat drops of rain began falling as Kristen made the turn of the driveway and disappeared out of sight. Jesse worked faster, trying his best to finish before the storm hit in full.

***

At 9:14 p.m., in heavy rain and fog, Kristin's Forerunner slammed head-on into an eighteen-wheeler fully loaded with lumber. The SUV—along with everything Jesse thought was worth living for—disintegrated in the blink of an eye, and then the remains caught fire.

There was nothing even left to cauterize.

Chapter 3

The Car

"Hello," he said into the phone on the nightstand next to the bed.

"Hello, Jesse, this is Molly from down the street. I didn't wake you, did I?"

"No," he yawned, "I had to get up and answer the phone anyway. What's the matter? Are your gutters clogged again?" He kicked his legs out of bed and, naked, headed in the direction of the bathroom.

"No, you did a great job cleaning them. Uh…last month when you were here you said if I ever wanted to sell my old car, I should call you first. Well, I'm calling."

Molly had to be in her eighties and owned a 1966 Buick Wildcat, which was in pretty good condition, kind of like its owner.

"What finally made you decide to sell it?"

"Well, you know gas is more than three dollars a gallon, and for that matter, bread is three dollars a loaf. And milk costs more than gas—it's over four dollars a gallon. And, well, my daughter, a big mucky-muck for a television network, says every time gas goes up, everything else does and…she's going to help me buy a new one."

"I didn't know you had a daughter," Jesse said, much more awake now.

"Oh, yes. She's flying in next week. She lives in New York. Well, anyway, while she's here she said she'd buy me a new Honda or Toyota. I don't know why I can't get a new Buick. But she says the Japanese cars…"

As Molly continued on and on, all Jesse could think of was New York City people. Yuck. New Yorkers were so pushy, but he did feel better about them since 9/11. He noticed the silence on the other end of the phone. "What did you say? I'm sorry, I must have stepped out."

"Out where?"

"It's just an expression."

"Expression. Oh. Okay, what I said was, are you still interested? In the car?"

"Yes, of course. I really would like to have the car," he said, while thinking, but not your pushy, executive, comes-with-whips-and-chains daughter.

"I thought maybe…"she paused, and then hurried on. "How about five hundred? It's almost an antique, you know."

"I was thinking more like seven-hundred fifty. I mean, since it is almost an antique."

"Well, if you think that's fair," she said, and he could hear the smile coming through the phone.

Before hanging up, they agreed that he'd pick up the car the following week. Afterward, he smiled as he thought there might be many things in his life that he would go to hell for, but cheating little old ladies wasn't going to be one of them.

***

Jesse walked the short half mile to Molly's house, the late afternoon October sunshine warm on his face. They lived in a country subdivision, and all the lots were at least five acres and heavily forested with oaks and pines mixed with a few cedars. The expected heavy winter rains usually did not start pouring until November, when they'd bring many of the pine and cedar needles down. The oak leaves would start to fall when they damn sure felt like it. There was no need to worry about Molly's gutters for a while.

Molly's shiny new car was parked in the center of her circular driveway.

"I thought you said you were going to buy a Honda," Jesse said as Molly came out the front door. He thought she must have been watching for him.

"Well, I had such good luck with my other car I just couldn't see changing horses in the middle of the race, so to speak."

He started walking around, admiring the new Buick sitting proudly in front of her house.

"Another red one, huh? I've always liked red for a car."

"Red is the only color car you should ever buy. It's just such an exciting color, don't you know?" She had a big smile spread across her face. "You need to smell the inside. There's nothing quite as magnificent as that new-car smell." She opened the car door.

Jesse ducked in and took a deep whiff. "You're so right. It does smell wonderful." When he straightened back up she handed him the title to the Wildcat.

"I never realized you spelled your name M-a-l-i-e," he said, reading her name off the paper.

"Oh, yes, but it's pronounced just like Molly, which is so much easier for most people." She had a wizened look that only older folks seemed able to fashion.

He reached into his pocket and handed her the check for the Wildcat.

"I would have been happy with five hundred," she said, looking at the check.

"It's okay, I have more dollars than sense," he joked as they started to walk around the corner of her house to the garage. He saw the Wildcat and, through the glass in the back window a faded stuffed animal, a tiger.

He gestured at the tiger. "You forgot to take out your friend."

"He's been in the car ever since I bought it. He's good luck. I couldn't possibly take him out now," she said, a small tear coming to her eye.

"I'll try to take good care of him." Jesse ducked his head and quickly changed the subject. "You didn't have to wash it."

"I didn't; my daughter did. In fact, where is that girl? I wanted you to meet her. She probably has the phone stuck in her ear, the big mucky-muck. I'll go get her."

Malie disappeared around the corner of the house. He looked

hard at what he'd just bought and started thinking of the profound implications of it all. It had taken many lonely years to summon the courage to begin doing what he'd determined was his destiny.

"So are you going to restore it or turn it into a Demolition Derby car?" a lovely voice behind him asked.

He turned around and saw Malie's daughter for the first time. It felt like slow motion. He could hardly believe his eyes. She was trip-over-your-tongue gorgeous. Her hair was a soft brown with more natural highlights than a rainbow. Short and slender, she had all the right stuff swelling out in all the right places. Her light-blue sleeveless top was the same color as her dramatic eyes, and she was wearing a short, pink skirt that showed off her athletic, naturally tanned legs.

"You're the mucky-muck?" he asked, not recognizing his own voice and wondering if she caught how stunned he was.

"I'm Kaikalina," she said giving him her hand, the scent of her perfume drifting by.

He reached out and took her hand. It was warm. All he could manage was, "Kaikalina?"

"Yeah, Kaikalina. It's Hawaiian for *sea* like my eyes and *pure* like my heart. Pretty original, huh? Just like me." Her smile glowed like an angel's halo. "My friends call me Leena. You can, too."

"Leena," he said, letting her name slip gently off his tongue. "No, what I meant was, uh…Did I hear correctly that you're Malie's daughter? You seem more like a granddaughter."

She still had that big smile on her pretty face when she said, "My mom is getting old. She's eighty-two and had me late in life. She was thirty-eight when I was born." When she saw him looking down, she said, "Let me save you the trouble. I'm forty-four and I'm not married." She held up her left hand.

"You New Yorkers are so direct, aren't you?"

"It's a learned defensive skill, but I'm not from the East Coast. We moved here from San Jose when I was thirteen."

"So you're a local."

"Well, I did graduate from Sutter Creek High before I moved

on to college in Palo Alto. So does five years make me a local?"
She put her hands on her hips.

"Local enough." He noted her stance and the tilt of her head.
"You must be extraordinarily smart if you graduated from Stanford.
And I'm Jesse Christenson. I live four houses down the street."

She surprised him by saying, "I know who you are. You're the
nice, handsome, but lonely, man from just down the street. What?"
She smiled, catching the look on his face. "You do go to the same
church as my mom," she added as Malie walked back around the
corner of the house toward them. "I've also seen you from the
window when you jog. Mom pretty much gives me the lowdown
on everything that goes on up here in the mountains."

"So you two have met, I see," Malie said with a warm grin.

"Mom, I think he's going to turn it into a derby car," Leena
said mischievously.

"No, no," he said, shaking his head.

"So you're going to restore it?"

He continued to shake his head, suddenly quiet.

"It's his car. He can do what he wants with it, honey," Malie said.

"So what *are* you going to do with it?" Leena persisted.

"It's a long story." Jesse's voice was barely a whisper.

"Why don't you stay for dinner and tell us about it?" Malie
asked. "We're barbecuing."

"Perhaps another time," he replied.

"Come on, stay for dinner," Leena said, oh so sweetly. "I promise
I won't bug you about the car. Scout's honor." She held three fingers
up together. "I might bug you about something else, but your car
secret is safe from me."

"How can I refuse an invitation when it's put that way?" he
said, meaning it. "But I would like to take the car home first, if you
don't mind?"

Jesse drove the Wildcat home, parked it in the middle of the
garage—a special place of honor—hurriedly closed the door, and
headed into the house. He was excited, and it had been a long time
since he'd been excited about anything. Was it the new car or the

girl? Probably both, he decided. He put on a clean shirt and brushed his teeth. He hadn't brushed his teeth in the middle of the afternoon since…a long time ago. He dismissed the thought.

Once again he walked to Malie's house, this time a little more briskly, and up to the front door. Leena opened it before he could knock.

"I knew you'd come back," she said, letting her breath out as if she had just finished running. "Mom, I told you he'd change his shirt," she yelled out to Malie, who was on the back deck turning the tri-tip steak.

"You're a brat. Observant, but still a brat," he said. "Wait a minute, you have on jeans, and before you had on a pink skirt."

"You did notice. You passed the test." She turned around in front of him. "How does my butt look in them?" She laughed. "You should see the look on your face. Come on, let's go out back." She took his hand and led him outside.

All he could think of was one word. Great.

The food was great and the evening was great and it passed very quickly. They got Malie talking and, like many intelligent older people who have not yet faded, she told great, diverse stories about how the world had changed before her eyes, in her lifetime. She repeated many times that change was the only certainty in life. Jesse and Leena talked about many things, especially about her work in New York. She actually was an important executive with World Cable Network, WCN. She'd been working there since its inception more than ten years before.

When she wanted to know about his life, Jesse said as little as possible and diverted the conversation back to her. He could see that changing the subject did not fool her.

"I know I promised, but would you tell me about the car?" Leena begged.

"Hey, you gave me the Scout's honor thing."

"So? I was never a Girl Scout. I just wanted you to come to dinner."

"Like I said, it's a long story." He looked first at Leena and then at her mom. Some kind of unspoken communication passed between the two of them.

"Maybe another time would be better," Leena said.

"It's starting to get late and you really don't have time to hear it if you're flying out tomorrow," Malie said.

"You're leaving tomorrow?" he asked, looking at Leena

"My flight leaves at noon. I have to be back to work in New York the following morning."

"Where are you flying from? Sacramento?" he asked, looking at each face. Both women nodded. "You know"—he rubbed his chin with his right hand and focused on Leena, staring deep into those baby blues—"I have to go down to Sacramento tomorrow, anyway. Why don't you let me take you to the airport? That way your mom doesn't have to drive you all that way."

Before she could answer, Malie said, "You see, honey? I told you he was a nice man."

He knew then he'd been had.

Leena looked at him seriously. "I'm pretty precious cargo, but I'll let you take me on one condition: that you tell me what you're going to do with the car."

She certainly was persistent, but after spending the evening with these two marvelous women there was something else about her, Jesse realized. Something he hadn't felt in a very long time. Trust. Only one other time had he felt that from the get-go. Now it was his turn to look serious. He just nodded yes. He could hear thunder crashing inside his head…or it might have been his heart.

Chapter 4

The Foundation

It was still early morning when the sound of his doorbell aroused Jesse from his reading.

"Did you dream of me?" Leena asked when he opened the front door. "I bet you forgot you're taking me to the airport."

"I thought we didn't have to leave for a few more hours," he said, avoiding her first question.

"We don't have to leave until ten-ish. I wanted to stop by while I was on my walk to see if you're a slob, or what." Smiling, she ducked beneath his arm and walked inside the house. "Thanks for inviting me in."

"Sure, uh...come in," he said, glancing around to see if he had picked up after himself.

"Not bad. I'm impressed. You're pretty tidy for a man." Looking around, she walked through the foyer and kicked off her clogs on the tile before she stepped down onto the thick carpet in the sunken living room. She walked over to peer up at the pictures on the wall next to the fireplace. "I thought you'd be watching television."

"I don't watch much TV," he said.

"Don't tell me you don't lie around and watch sports and drink beer," she said with a sparkle in her eye. "What do you do in your spare time?"

"Come here, and I'll show you." He led her through the kitchen and into his study.

"Wow, what a library. You have thousands of—have you read all these books?" He nodded as she reached for a textbook on one of the many shelves from the bookcase that ran from floor to ceiling. "Electrical engineering? Most of these are textbooks." She turned to look at him.

"I never finished college, and many years ago I thought it a good idea to get my degree at home. I got the course catalogs from some of the best schools in America, and then I bought the textbooks and did all the exercises at home."

"Why didn't you just go online or apply to some of the schools?"

"I'm not exactly a classroom type of guy." Jesse shrugged. "Besides, I've read all these books and understand the information. Isn't that why you go to school in the first place?"

"There are other benefits—"

"Yeah, I know, like networking, making valuable contacts, giving to the alumni association. Look, I figure I've earned the equivalent of a couple of doctorates. And I really don't care if anyone recognizes me for that or not." He saw the puzzled look on her face. "It's just how I am. Hey, you want a cup of coffee?"

"Thanks, not right now. I just wanted to see if you're for real." She stared deeply into his eyes as if she were trying to see into his soul.

"Did I pass the test?" He hoped she'd say yes.

"Maybe. We'll see," she said, strolling back to the foyer, stopping only to slip her shoes back on. "Don't forget me." And just like a breeze blowing effortlessly through an open door, she went out the same way she came in, leaving only the delicate scent of her essence behind.

* * *

Jesse drove his pick-up truck, a Dodge Diesel 4x4, to Malie's house. He felt like he was picking up his very first date. The women were both outside waiting for him. This time Leena was dressed like an executive, wearing a smart, dark-blue, pinstriped suit. Her skirt was still cut short, showing her legs, but her cleavage had disappeared behind her tailored, buttoned-up blouse. She had one small bag and a briefcase on the ground next to her and held the strap of her black leather purse in her right hand. Jesse got out and hurried around to open the door for her.

"That's a lost art these days," Leena said. "The only time men open a door for me now is if they stick out their hand for a tip.

Malie just smiled.

"I'm one of the last true gentlemen left, if you broadly interpret that term." Jesse stuck out his hand and said, "To help you up, of course."

"Get the bags," she said, sounding like a New York City woman. Leena was still laughing as she hugged Malie goodbye. "I'll call when I get in."

"You always do." Malie turned to Jesse. "She's a good girl. Always has been."

It was a ninety-minute drive to the airport, unless they hit an unexpected traffic snarl. The road he lived on was only about a mile from the main highway. They covered it in silence.

"You're going to make me ask you again, aren't you?" Leena finally asked.

He looked over at her. It was a nice view. She was staring straight through him.

"Curious or pushy?" he asked.

"Probably both. Are you one of those moody types?"

"Not normally, it's just that this subject…I only told one other person about this idea, and she was killed on the same day."

"Oh, you mean your wife." He jerked his head around to look at her. "Mom. Church. There are no secrets in church."

He didn't say anything for a few minutes. He could feel her eyes on him and felt something else passing between them, something he hadn't felt since the last time he brushed his teeth twice the same morning.

"You remind me of her." He glanced at Leena. She wore a soft, almost sad smile. She put her hand on top of his. He sighed and said, "I had a dream thirteen years ago. It wasn't like any other dream I've ever had, then or since. It was solid and complete, almost like a complete set of plans was inserted into my brain in the middle of the night. I told my wife about it over breakfast. I finished telling her at a little past nine in the morning. A short twelve hours later, she was gone…dead. I've lived that same morning over and over for thirteen years now."

"Your house doesn't look like a shrine."

"No, probably not. My shrine is inside my heart."

"So you think it was your fault?"

"No. Well, yes. Look. My dream, my idea, is not evil. In fact, just the opposite, but I'm worried that somehow evil is attracted to it, like wolves to a newborn baby left out in the snow."

When he looked back over at her, she was just looking at him. He had to look away as he negotiated a series of turns on the highway.

"I'm not a newborn babe. I'm not afraid," she said when she finally spoke. "I'm a lot tougher than I look."

When he finished negotiating the series of curves, he looked once again into her eyes. They almost had a pleading quality to them. He turned the last corner in his mind. "If I tell you…you have to promise not to tell anyone until I say it's okay."

She put her hand tenderly on his face and once again he turned to look her in the eyes.

"I promise," she said with all the solemnity of a wedding vow.

Jesse felt a huge weight lift. "Okay, then: the Take-Us, that's what I call my idea." She furrowed her brow. "I gave it that name because it will take us to the store, or the city, or anywhere we want to go. Take us away. In its simplest form, it's an electric car, but it's so much more. It's actually a self-contained producer of electrical energy."

"What do you mean, self-contained?"

"As it travels down the road, its own motive power generates the energy it needs to keep it going. It never has to stop and refuel or recharge, as long as you keep it above the threshold speed."

"So it doesn't have batteries?"

"Sure, it has batteries. They're only for initial momentum, though. In fact, that's where all the other people have failed when they've invented electric cars. Their cars were only users of electricity. My idea is to create it. At first I only saw it as a car, but as I thought about it for all these years I realized that if you were to drive the Take-Us to your garage, raise the rear wheels, put it on cruise control and then plug it into your house, you could power your entire house…within limits."

"Is this just theoretical?"

"Powering the house, yes, but look." He put the truck into neutral, and it kept going down the highway, friction barely slowing it. "You see," he said as he put it back in gear, "it's a law that objects in motion tend to stay in motion. Well, I've found a way to use that motion to create motive power."

"That's all well and fine, but everybody knows that friction will eventually stop everything."

"I found a way to work around it, to actually work with it as long as you remember it's still just a machine and needs routine maintenance. Like all autos, some parts will break or wear out."

"You mean you already have a working model?" she asked, amazed.

"Yes, I do."

She sat silent for a moment or two. "So why do you need Mom's car?"

"It will be my first large prototype."

"So what did you build first, a go-cart?" she asked, placing her fingers an inch apart.

"No, larger."

"A Volkswagen?" She spread her fingers a few inches farther apart.

"Size isn't everything."

"What are you talking about?"

"What are you thinking about?"

She burst out laughing, and it sounded like ice tinkling in a glass to a man stranded in a desert for thirteen long years. It sounded so wonderful that he laughed right along with her.

"Really, what is it?" she asked.

"A golf cart. I built it three years ago and I drive it to and around the golf course three or four days a week. I haven't charged the batteries in all that time."

"So it does work. You've lived up here, what…ten years?"

"Twelve."

"And you had this idea all that time. So why did you wait so long to pursue it?"

"Honestly, I kept hoping that someone else would invent it. I finally realized this was such a big idea that, well, even with all the years of studying—"

"That's what the textbooks are all about."

"Yeah, that's a big part of it. But anyhow," he said, hurrying on, "I know I'm not smart enough to have created it, and the only possibility is that God gave the burden to me to carry."

She sat quietly, thinking of what he said. "It will change your life drastically. Is that what you're afraid of?"

"It's not that I'm afraid for myself."

"Then who? Think of how much life will be improved for everybody. We won't have to kiss ass to all those countries in the Middle East anymore. No more brownouts. And we won't be at the mercy of big oil companies. Anybody, anywhere on earth, will be able to have electricity. The quality of air will—" When she saw him staring at her she stopped. "What?"

"So let's see. Who would be pissed at that?" He put one finger up. "One, all the Middle East countries." Two fingers up. "Two, all the big electricity providers." Three fingers. "Three, all the big oil companies like Shell, Exxon, and wait, how about British Petroleum, Venezuela, Mexico, and let's not forget Russia." Another finger. "Four, ever heard of global warming? If the air were suddenly cleaned up, how many people in that crowd would lose jobs, grants, and agendas for political change?"

"You're running out of fingers."

"I've got a thumb left. When all these different entities see their source of income drying up, they'll start looking crookedly at their neighbors, and wars will start again. I've thought this through for a long time."

"Lots of enemies, huh? I've got some catching up to do."

"You don't know the half of it," he said. You know I'm a Christian, right?"

She nodded.

"Well, Christians like me believe in the one God of peace and love. If radical Muslims believe in a different God, as they interpret their Quran—well, you can look around and see the terrible carnage their Allah is creating right now, here on earth—then I guess you could safely say I probably have another billion or so enemies. And the radical-Islamic God of Evil is after me, too."

They were just exiting off the freeway and onto the road to the airport when Leena said, "So what's the plan?"

"You have to understand there will be new wars that start, and many people will die because of my idea or, rather, invention."

"Isn't progress always like that?"

"Progress won't be responsible for the dead bodies. I will." He looked straight ahead. "But I have to build it."

She was still looking at his face and could make out the pain and utter sincerity. "I understand that. But how you debut it and how you protect yourself has to go hand-in-hand."

He nodded as he pulled up to the unloading zone.

She reached into her purse. "Here's my card. It has my phone numbers on it. Try my cell first. I always have it with me. Call me next week. I'll have some time to talk then. Maybe we can come up with a plan."

"Leena, listen. Please. You don't have to get involved in any of this."

She looked in his eyes and said, "I already am. Remember, I promised. Besides, you don't have anybody else." She leaned over and softly touched her lips to his. "I've got to hurry. Don't forget. Call me next week."

He watched her walk directly into the airport, wanting to shout out one more time not to say anything to anyone about the car because it would probably get him, or her, or more likely both of them killed. But, somehow he thought she already knew that.

Chapter 5

The Take-Us

Jesse opened the garage door after returning from church and inspected the Wildcat. It had been nine days since he bought it. Attending church was the first break he allowed himself to take during the sixteen-hour days he'd been working, stripping the car all the way down to the bare frame.

He hadn't attended church as a kid or even in his twenties or thirties. In fact, he hadn't been baptized until he was forty-nine. The priest, Father Mark, asked why it took so long for him to find his way, and in a candid moment of honesty Jesse said, "It took a long time before I realized that God wasn't mad at me. If you knew what I did in the war…Well, I just didn't think I would be welcome here."

Father Mark had peered through him as if he were gazing at his naked soul and said, "You've been given a shiny new soul. Don't get it dirty."

What surprised Jesse more than anything is that neither the priest nor anyone else had ever asked him exactly what he'd done that was so bad.

Even forgiven, he would need all the help God could send him to bring this assigned task to fruition. And the biggest problem was that he couldn't speak of it to anyone without having them think he was some kind of weirdo. Some things just needed to stay buried under the cold earth.

He climbed into his coveralls and resumed his work converting the car. While working on mundane things like removing this rusty clamp on the muffler, his mind rolled along, mostly in reverse.

When his wife was taken—No. He'd stopped saying that many years ago. She died. There was a settlement, and he'd received a significant amount, two million dollars. He'd sold and moved from the house that stopped being a home. The memories there were as thick as the trees in the forests that surrounded it, and he recognized, through all the pain and anguish, that if he stayed there he'd slowly—or in a moment of quiet desperation—perish. There was no sleep to be had on many a night, just a long, gray wait for dawn. Days with no end that only brought out either a silent or a real scream of loneliness. He recognized he'd been lonely his entire adult life. The only exception was the few short years he'd been married. Only then had he felt complete and whole.

The clamp came loose suddenly and the muffler bonked him on the head. It hurt, but not like the hurt in his heart going through the long desert of grief.

He had plenty of money in the bank, which had allowed him to pay for a house up front. Occasionally, mostly just to get out and about, he'd pick up small jobs, making sure he was always paid in cash. He had no open credit and hoped that it appeared he'd fallen off the face of the earth. He continued to study nonstop, the car fighting for its own space, always in the front of his mind.

He'd been lonely and made few friends in Vietnam. Those friends he did make became as close as lovers on a one-night stand. If the morning came and you never saw them again, at least you'd had one night of comfort. They were all brothers, comrades in arms, who were constantly put in impossible situations, fighting, bleeding, and celebrating. Celebrating the death of their enemies, not in a gloating way, but happy that they were the ones still standing and breathing. Just to continue breathing one more day was the only goal. When a comrade went away, never to be heard from again, each man had a way of hardening or numbing himself. Soon all feelings shriveled up and died. The men became like the walking dead. Some were killed, some wounded, and some just did their time and rotated back to the World. The World—that's what they called home sweet home, America. It became their only reality.

Hidden Truths

The nature of the war in Vietnam was deeply personal. They each came to the war not as a unit but more like castaways who washed up on a deserted island one at time. Most combat veterans never joined or attended any sort of reunion of their old outfits. Most were not joiners of anything. They were so unpopular when they returned home that most just tried to forget it ever happened. He believed more soldiers had died after they came home—by outright suicide or on the installment plan of drugs and alcohol—than were killed by the enemy. They developed skills that had been forged in the cauldron of battle and internalized, a never-to-be forgotten part of them, especially the ability to see the world in a more glowing white or absolute black, life or death, less in shades of pale gray moonlight.

Jesse came out from under the car and saw his eyes reflected in the chrome of the rear bumper sitting on the floor. He could see in them the pain and suffering and deprivation that certain memories brought, in the same way that a bucket dipped in a deep, dark, stagnant well brings up only foulness. That suffering, often visible in the eyes of combat veterans, was the reason he never went to reunions. After he came home, Jesse never saw any of the men in his old unit again.

He stood up, looked outside at the beautiful fall day, and dismissed his thoughts, commanding them to go back to the private hell where they belonged.

* * *

Jesse received a package from FedEx the next day, a cell phone from Leena. Her enclosed note said it would work anywhere and that he should call her on it rather than use his home phone. He thought that was a little over-the-top and told her so when he called.

"So are you calling me on it right now?"

He ignored her question because he knew she already knew the answer. "So who's paying for this?"

"I set up an account at the network, as a developing story. They love new stories, and it always keeps the bean counters happy.

Although it really doesn't matter since my boss likes me and signs anything I put in front of his face. In effect, I approve the budgets in my department."

"So now I'm going to be a story."

"I really don't know yet. I'm still thinking about it, but what can it hurt for now? You convinced me with the fingers thing."

"I just don't want to get you into trouble."

"You mean like knocking me up or something?" She laughed aloud. "I'm a little too old for that, and you're a little too late. Of course, if you did, my mom would be ecstatic." Another laugh and then she continued. "This isn't that unusual. And incidentally, we never spoke about any kind of time frame when you would be finished with the…uh…your prototype?"

"Pressure, pressure." Her innuendo about sex painted the word *betrayer* inside his head.

"Relax, there is no pressure. I just wanted a ball-park guesstimate."

"It should be within six months, sometime in the spring. Maybe earlier. I started making the special components years ago, but I'll have to get some different machining done and some other stuff I can't do by myself. You're never sure how other shops' schedules are going to be, but since I pay cash, I usually go to the front of the line."

"Can you really do this all by yourself?"

"Call me in six months and I'll let you know." He immediately wanted to put those words back in his stupid mouth.

"How about in a couple of days instead?" she asked, sounding more like the executive she was. "I'm going to Washington, the D.C. one, tonight to set up an interview with the new Secretary of Homeland Security."

They talked for a little while longer and then hung up. Jesse breathed a sigh of relief that she had already begun to consider their security implications. He needed to be more concerned about getting the car built and decided there was nothing to worry about until the grand Take-Us debut. They had to have their security ready at that time. He didn't know what he should do about the lockbox on his heart.

* * *

Five months after he started working on her, the Wildcat/Take-Us was nearly finished. Under his knowing touch, the cold steel and hard copper wire, seemed to vibrate with the very essence of life. Jesse could almost feel the throb of energy coursing through the many wires, like blood through veins. It was his labor of love, though he had no feeling of labor. He'd had to remove many components, such as the engine and transmission—the Wildcat's heart and lungs. The newly rebuilt rear wheels each had its own motor and were markedly superior. Each would capacitate a much higher degree of performance. The existing fourteen-inch wheels and tires had been replaced with new, twenty-inch, low-profile wheels, resulting in a larger contact patch for higher performance. He'd also stiffened the suspension with new gas shocks and heavier springs to accommodate the extra weight of the batteries.

This first large-scale prototype didn't have air conditioning or a heater, but since it would be late spring before he was finished, those things shouldn't matter. Jesse figured the absence of power-steering would be kind of a bitch, making it difficult to steer at low speed. He'd easily found and purchased from "off the shelf" many of the main components used to build the drive system. The car had pretty much ceased being a Buick Wildcat and had been transformed into the Take-Us.

Jesse's cell phone buzzed; he did not consider it a ring. He wiped the grime and blood from his hands as he came out from under the car.

"Hello, who is this?" he demanded.

"You are so funny! Who else has this phone number?" Leena asked, with a laugh in her voice. She was always laughing. They spoke at least three times a week, often more. He really liked her phone voice; it always sounded so fresh. And whether by design or not, she made him feel like he was the only thing on her mind.

"Nobody."

"What's wrong? You doing okay?" she asked, concern apparent.

"Yeah, I'm fine, just a little tired. Why?"

"Something in your voice…I thought that since you're getting so close to finishing, maybe you're feeling a little pressured. By the way, it's okay for someone to worry about you."

"Not pressured, just incredibly busy. This three-pronged approach is so complex I don't have a minute to myself. But you don't have to worry about me. I'm a big boy."

"I'll worry if I choose," she admonished. "You are no longer in this alone, remember?"

"Sorry. You're right." He opened the fridge and pulled out a cold Coors, taking a deep swallow. "I need to get rid of this tunnel vision. How's it going on your end?"

"I've got the New York City contacts and that part handled. Just keep feeding me all the info you write, and you can cross that part of the project off your list. Is the security thing going well?"

"Probably as well as can be expected. I don't think the neighbors have a clue. It's probably overkill."

She seemed to accept that without question, which was rare. "You know you don't have to hurry on the car. We can do this later in the year or even next year."

"It'll be just as dangerous later as it is now. I not only want to, but I need to get it over with. I wonder if Henry Ford had to worry about any of this kind of stuff in his day."

"I don't know about Ford, but I know another guy who changed the world, and he paid the price."

"Oh, who was that?"

"Jesus."

He laughed. "You could compare me to many things, mostly the back end of certain farm animals, but Jesus?"

"You are both instruments of change. The world will be better because of you."

"A friend of mine once told me to imitate Jesus, be humble. Instead of becoming a carpenter, I became an ironworker. It paid better…Come on, that was just a little joke."

"Whatever. You're too close to it. Others will see it for what it is," Leena said, her voice full of conviction.

* * *

Jesse was ready to test-drive the Take-Us for the first time at the end of April. He had "rolled the wheels" while it was up on the jack stands, but that was different. Leena wouldn't be there for the test drive. She was in Europe on business. That was okay with him because if it didn't work or something worse happened, like he crashed, at least he'd be the only victim. He'd always believed that if he killed himself doing something crazy, that was okay. But it would be an unforgivable sin to take anyone out with him.

He lowered the jack, and the car settled on the concrete floor. He ran his hand over it one more time. The garage door was open and he glanced around to see if anyone was taking undue notice. He was alone. He climbed in, closed the car door, and put the seatbelt on. He pushed the buttons to lower all the windows—they still ran off the batteries—and pulled on his new, soft, black-leather driving gloves, purchased just for the occasion. He looked into the mirror, adjusted his hat one last time, and saw his friend, the tiger, in the back window.

"You ready?" No answer. Perfect. He took a deep breath and put the car in reverse, gently pushing the accelerator down. The Take-Us moved slowly backward. He imagined it looked like one of those big aircraft carriers that some lady breaks a champagne bottle over as it slowly, but with ever increasing speed, heads out to sea for the first time.

He stopped just short of the street in case it wouldn't go into forward—there were only three choices: reverse, neutral, and forward, no gears. He needn't have worried; it moved flawlessly forward. It was smooth and quiet, just like his golf cart, only much bigger. He drove around the neighborhood and never accelerated over twenty miles per hour, he hoped—he still hadn't figured out how to hook up a speedometer. Speedometers are connected to the transmissions of modern cars, and since the Take-Us had no transmission, there was no way of telling how fast it was going.

The car handled well. It tucked into the tight corners, hugging them snuggly, and then emerged with no sway at all. It had been a lot of work to re-engineer and install disc brakes and the computer controller he had invented to monitor the braking process. When the brakes were applied, it increased the electric motor's natural resistance to slow the car down tremendously. When he stomped hard on the brakes, they worked more efficiently than any modern automobile. That feature would take some time to get used to. It was fine as long as he didn't do anything crazy, like emergency braking with another car close on his tail. The follower would never be able to stop in time and would plow into him.

Having previously decided that he would only drive for about fifteen minutes, he figured he must have been in a time warp. Never had time seemed to pass so quickly. He was so constrained on the drive, trying to hear and feel everything, that when he returned home he suddenly let out a scream of victory.

"It works, it really works!"

For most of his life, there was no one around to hear Jesse's sudden bursts of emotion, and the same was true of this occasion. He pulled the car back into the garage and did a thorough inspection. It didn't look like anything had fallen off, so it was time to take it farther and faster.

* * *

It had been a month since his first test drive. Jesse waved to Malie as he drove past her house. She was out front washing her new car. Since he'd finally met Leena, Malie called regularly with projects that needed doing. She had a key to the church and put him to work repairing minor things. Like a mother-in-law, she was always finding things to keep him busy.

His smile slowly dissolved when he remembered this would be the longest and most difficult test drive to date.

There was no straightaway longer than half a mile in the mountains where he lived. When he finally drove down into the valley, he accelerated to something over 120 miles per hour where the road was flat and straight. He had resolved the speedometer problem by adapting a motorcycle speedometer. It was somewhat accurate at lower speeds, but was suspect at high speed, registering all the way up to two hundred miles per hour.

Once again, the Take-Us was the smoothest and quietest car he'd ever been in. When he came back from the eight-hour test drive, he was confident he could drive the Take-Us all the way to New York City without any problems. He'd make the drive beginning next week. He had to finish a couple more projects dealing with security and take a few more test-drives. He felt new and invigorated. New beginnings are like that.

The Take-Us was ready for the great debut.

Now the only question remaining was, was he?

***

He began the three-thousand mile journey to the east coast on June 2, a bright Monday morning. He had a week to get to New York.

On the second day, he reached a flat straight stretch of road on Interstate 80 in Nevada, adjacent to the world-famous Bonneville Salt Flats. Since there were no other cars in sight, he decided to see how fast the Take-Us would go.

Jesse started accelerating, and the only thing he heard was the sound of the air rushing by and the barely perceptible, distant whine of the electrics. When he reached the speed of 181 miles per hour, he started to back off. He was jazzed. He knew, from his own calculations, that 180 miles per hour was about sixty percent of theoretical capability. But knowing something intellectually and going that fast are two very different perceptions. His adrenaline level was red-lining almost off the chart.

He remembered the first time he'd gone that fast on a motorcycle. He'd been riding a new BMW K-1000 with some friends, all of them heading to a bar. On a long stretch of laser-beam straight road, he got a bug up his ass and yelled, "Hey, I wonder how fast this bike will go? Look for me in one of the ditches, or I'll see you at the bar." He dropped a gear, crouched low over the tank and sped off, his eyes rattling like a 10.0 earthquake as he watched the speedometer reach 180. The telephone poles went by like pickets on a fence. When he'd started to slow down, he'd been very conscious of the wind rushing by. If he'd been sitting up straight, the force of the wind would have ripped him right off the motorcycle. He arrived at the bar long before the rest of his buddies. He had such an adrenaline high he couldn't stop talking.

Sometime later, he realized why drug-users were drug-users. Maybe when the druggies said, "I have a need for speed," it came from that fabulous feeling of going so fast. Jesse figured they just picked the wrong kind of speed. Meth was a definite death sentence waiting to happen.

Luckily, he slowed the Take-Us at that moment, reluctantly leaving the sweet feeling of speed. A Utah state trooper was traveling from the other direction a few minutes later. As they passed each other, the cop eyeballed him hard. His radar had probably picked up the Take-Us long before he could see it. Jesse figured the cop was probably thinking, "That old car couldn't have been going that fast."

The rest of the trip back East was slow and uneventful, but soul-searchingly satisfying. Jesse spent his free hours each evening poring over potential problems and seeking out the slightest anomaly, like a detective searching for clues. He found nothing of interest, at least with the car.

Day One

Chapter 6

Road Trip

The following Monday morning, Jesse found Leena waiting for him outside WCN headquarters in New York City. There were two camera crews set up, filming the Take-Us car as he pulled up to the curb.

Leena spoke into the microphone while she opened the passenger door. "This is Mr. Jesse Christenson, inventor of this new type of automobile. So how was the ride here?"

"So far, so good. Why don't you get in and join me? You can find out for yourself."

"I think I'll do that." She faced the mounted camera outside. "I've been invited on an adventure," she said into the microphone as she slid into the front seat, one hand grasping her short skirt to keep it from hiking any farther up, showing just the right amount of TV leg. "So where are we off to?"

"I thought San Francisco would suffice," Jesse said as Leena held the mike in front of his lips.

"So let me and all of our viewers understand this. We're going all the way to San Francisco, California, without stopping for gas. Is that your plan?"

"Absolutely, we're taking a long road trip to demonstrate the capabilities of this next generation automobile, and you will be the independent witness."

Leena turned to look back outside, where the camera was located, and said, "Yes. I've agreed to go along and document this historic journey. Over the next five days and three thousand miles, I'll be reporting on this new, exciting, technology that will change our world if all goes according to plan. This is Leena Delaney reporting 'On the Road.'...Did you get all that?" she asked, listening though the tiny earphone inside her right ear. "Okay, good." She put down the microphone and looked at Jesse. "Let's go."

He looked back. "What did you mean by saying 'if' we get there?"

"Building suspense. Are you up for this?"

"Never up, never in," he said.

"Excuse me?"

"Golf term. It means—"

"I can figure out what it means. Are you sure it's not a pocket-pool term?" She laughed. "So, really, how are you?"

He once again felt her trying to see deep into his soul. "Great," he said softly. "It's really good to see you again."

"You, too." She smiled and put her hand on top of his. "How about the car?"

"You need not be worried. It's been a really good trip so far, absolutely no problems." He removed his hand from under hers and put his sunglasses on. "I thought you were going to get one of those news bunnies to do the on-air stuff."

"I got my start by being one of those bunnies."

"I meant no offense. I think it's a great idea to use pretty girls to read the news. It takes something that is inherently bad, sometimes even evil, and makes it more palatable."

"I think it's a great idea, too," she said with a great, big, all-teeth television smile. "In fact, it was my idea from the start. All the other networks had all these old battle-axes reading the news. They might have been good reporters but were horrible to look at. TV is visual. Reporters gather, readers read. That's one of the reasons why I was promoted into the job I now have."

"From reporter to big honcho?"

"I used to be a reporter, a damn good one, actually, but the route wasn't quite so straight. The ladder had a few bends in it."

"Bends are good for the soul."

"Yeah, yeah, but on a more serious note, you need to understand I am committed to this story, and I believe in your dream." She put her hand back on top of his and gave it a little squeeze. "I always planned to go with you, and I thought it best that I do the on-air stuff. Besides, I really do need a little fun time off."

"Thanks," he said, uncomfortable under her gaze. "Is traffic always this bad?"

"Just be happy we're getting out before rush hour. That's when it really gets crazy."

"The air here stinks."

"It's the city. It's supposed to stink."

"Supposed to stink. Ya think? I guess that's how our mindsets are. When I think I can change this dirty old air into something so much better, well, it gets too unbelievable. It gets too big for me."

"I really do know what you mean. That's why it has to be taken one step at a time. If we try to solve it all right now, it would just overwhelm us both." She put a Southern drawl in her voice, and said, "So how 'bout lightening up a bit there, bub."

"You're probably right," he said, feeling himself smile at the "we" and "us" in her last sentence. "Yikes, lady! What are you doing?"

She had her short skirt hiked up around her waist.

"Don't look now, but I'm on holiday. And it's way too beautiful a spring day to be stuck in these pantyhose. Besides, what's the big deal, underwear is about the same thing as a bikini bottom."

"Once a California girl, always a California girl," he said, trying to keep his eyes looking out the windshield. "Growing up in Indiana, spring was always my favorite season. I don't know what it was, but there was something about the annual renewal of fresh life that set my soul to singing, all those bright colors and chirping birds. It's such a sharp contrast to this bleak city. Spring seems to be saying to me that as long as the heart is beating, you will find hope."

"So you're an optimist."

"Optimist? Is that the same thing as a hope-ist? If so, that's me to a fault. As I've traveled the road through life, I've sometimes seen that mere existence tends to knock you down. I've been down so many times I have calluses on my knees from getting up," he said, laughing. "But it really doesn't matter how many times you're down. It seems to me your responsibility is to keep dragging yourself up by the chains your mind constantly tries to shackle you with. Sometimes it even feels like there's a chain-link fence that separates you from sanity and insanity."

"Sanity and insanity. You don't mean to say that everyone faces those in life?"

"Everyone. That's a blanket statement and normally you can never say anything that fits everybody, but in this case, well, I've seen bad things happen to good people and good things happen to bad people. Someone as pampered as a princess would see breaking a fingernail as a terrible crisis point in her life. And at that point she would have to make a decision either to let it go, or let it begin the task of destroying her."

"But at the time you don't really *decide* to destroy yourself. You just take the wrong fork in the road and end up at that fence you were talking about. Is that what you mean?"

"So you've been there, too?" He glanced at her, trying to see her expression.

She stared straight ahead. "Like you said, we all have been."

They were silent for a time. Leena reached down on the floorboard in front of her, brought out her laptop computer, and starting typing.

Eventually, they were out on the empty highway—at least it seemed empty compared to the city—and their spirits started to climb. Jesse tried to maintain a reasonable speed, but his spirits began soaring just like his speed.

After some time, Leena stopped typing and put her computer away. "This car is so quiet now. Did you know I learned to drive in this car?" she asked, making airplane movements with her right hand that was sticking out the window into the wind.

"I wondered about that."

"I was only four years old when Mom and Dad bought it. It was twenty-two miles one way to school. This old thing went up to our home and down the hill to school thousands of times. I was involved in everything: sports, drama, even cheerleading." She gave him a hugely exaggerated smile.

"Yeah, I can see the cheerleader in you."

"I got my driver's license when I was a junior in high school. My dad wouldn't let me take this car out with my friends at night. He said the back seat was too big, and I had to take our small Ford pickup. It had bucket seats."

"Smart man. What happened to your dad?"

"One night he told my mom he had a stomachache and couldn't sleep. Mom thought it was because his favorite team, Notre Dame, had just lost a big bowl game. That was January, 1995. Mom found him early the next morning, sitting in his favorite chair in the living room. He'd had a massive heart attack and died. We like to pretend he was asleep when it happened."

"It seems that no matter how hard I try, this conversation keeps going in a down direction. What's up with that?"

That brought about a quick and fleeting smile. "Don't worry about it. That was twelve years ago."

"Twelve years ago," he said, a wistful tone in his voice.

"Come on, let's stop up here at the next rest stop, find a good spot, and finish the shots we have to deal with now. Maybe then we can have a good road trip and get the rest of this adventure figured out," she said, all business.

Leena had decided she'd film the trip at various spots up until another crew met them in San Francisco for the conclusion. The network would hold the video files and then edit all the segments at the same time, releasing it as one complete story.

"This is Leena Delaney, 'On the Road,' accompanying Jesse Christenson across the country in his hi-tech Take-Us automobile. We are reporting live from a rest stop here on Interstate 80 in New Jersey. We left New York City several hours ago, and I can state personally, as well as professionally, that this new type of automobile is very impressive. Jesse, why don't you tell us something about your car?"

"Well, as you can see, this is a 1966 Buick Wildcat. I call this car the Take-Us, as in 'take us away from oil tyranny.' There are many different reasons I chose the Wildcat for my prototype. The first was its size. I needed the large trunk space to put in the power-generating equipment the car requires. The engine compartment now functions as the trunk." He pointed and Leena followed his hand with the camera into the cavernous, empty engine compartment and then to the batteries located at the very bottom of the compartment.

"Another reason," Jesse continued, "is that this car is not very aerodynamic and is much heavier than modern autos. Weight is one of the major factors of modern auto design because of the fuel efficiency factor. It takes more power to move more weight, and more power means more gas. That's probably why modern cars look so much alike." Leena filmed the exterior view of the car. "What that means is that if we can cross the entire country in this car without stopping for fuel, then auto designers would be free to design an auto in any shape they chose. There would be no limiting shape or weight factors."

"How is it possible not to stop for fuel?"

"The Take-Us is initially powered by battery, up to about twenty miles per hour, at which point the main source of energy is created. It also recharges the batteries as it runs. The vehicle is self-sustaining after the twenty-miles-per-hour point."

"How does that work?"

"Let me see if I can explain this without getting terribly complex." Jesse knelt down and pointed at the outside of the rear tire. "Every time this particular tire makes one complete revolution, the tire travels about ninety-one inches, or seven feet seven inches. That means this tire will have to turn about 696 times to travel one mile. If it did it in one minute that would mean it was turning at 696 revolutions per minute, called rpm. These rims are twenty inches in diameter, and have been specially modified for this car. They have a pulley system welded on the inside that you can't really see from this view. Belts run up to a number of different, specially modified alternators that have three-inch pulleys. That changes the gear ratio so that it's 6.33 to one. That means the alternators are spinning about six times faster than the rear wheels. And these special alternators have a clutch built in and produce eighty percent of their rated output at only 1,800 rpm. Another key component is the on-board computer with its unique power management system, as well as some other super-secret stuff," he said with a wry smile. "The bottom line is that once the Take-Us gets moving down the road at about twenty-five miles per hour, it's totally self-sustaining."

"Would this work in any other applications?" Leena asked as a big rig went growling by, vomiting black smoke into the air.

Jesse stood back up and pointed to the tractor-trailer. "I believe it would work very well in large trucks like that one. However, you'd still need a diesel motor to get up to speed before the electrics could take over. I think this would really work well on trains, but just like the trucks, you'd still need to get up to speed before it would work. I don't know anything about ships. Who knows?" He shrugged his shoulders and opened the passenger door, opened the glove box, and pointed to an ordinary household outlet installed in it. "What's very interesting that I do know, though, is that if you jack the back wheels up, you have an excess amount of electricity, perhaps enough to power your own home."

"Does that really work?" Leena asked, surprise apparent in her voice.

"Only when the rear wheels are turning. I'll be glad to show you as we're heading down the highway." He looked straight into the camera. "You brought a blow-dryer, didn't you?"

Instead of answering Leena stood in front of the Take-Us once again, training the camera on herself. "I will be going all the way to San Francisco, riding in and reporting on this car, the vehicle of the future with a strong tie to the past. Reporting live 'On the Road' for WCN, I'm Leena Delaney."

"This is going to be a great trip," Jesse said. "But before we get started, I gotta pee, and I suggest you do the same. I learned from the drive East that although the car has an unlimited range, it will only travel as far as your bladder can hold."

They had been driving for about an hour, chatting about nothing, when Leena tried to turn the radio on. "This thing work?"

"No, uh, well, it did kind of work, but I forgot to...well, I ran about eight hundred amps of power though it, and it just kind of sizzled." Jesse stumbled through an explanation, clearly embarrassed.

"So no music?" she asked, tilting her head and peering over her sunglasses.

"Sure, we have music. There's a boom box on the back seat. You just have to plug it into the outlet in the glove compartment."

"So that's why you put that in there," she said, with a knowing look. "I had forgotten about it. You mean that outlet actually works?"

"I wasn't kidding when I said you could run your blow dryer off it. The cops are gonna really love this car. They have enough trouble with women putting on their make-up while driving, and now women will be able to do their hair on the way to work, too."

"Some women are very busy and—"

"Don't forget they can make a fresh pot of coffee, and get a bagel out of the toaster and, I guess, get some cream cheese out of the refrigerator." Jesse was on a roll now and just couldn't stop himself.

"Oh, yeah, and men will be able to keep their beer cold on the way home from work."

"So you put on your make-up in the car?"

"And you drink beer in the car?"

"Oooh. I take the fifth," he said, letting go of the steering wheel and holding up both hands. "Have you ever heard of the law of unintended consequences?"

"Of course. I had a college professor once who gave a great example of it."

"Like what?"

"If I can remember correctly, he stated that life insurance, which most people agree is a pretty good thing, creates the opposite result at times instead of protecting the insured. If they were never listed on the policy, they might still be alive. No one would have profited from their death, but they were worth more dead than alive after taking out the policy. Total opposite of what was intended."

"Yeah, that's sort of what I'm talking about. What kind of un-intended things are going to happen because of the invention of the Take-Us car? How about if a woman did try to blow-dry her hair while driving, hit a school bus, and killed a bunch of kids? Would that be my fault?"

"You can't think of it in those terms."

"Why not? I don't think it would be a good thing to hide your head in a paper bag and plead stupidity."

"Do you think the guy who invented the baseball bat really thought somebody would rob a liquor store with it? People can subvert anything. That's the nature of our species. You can never stop the advancement of humanity just because of it. Besides, for every bad outcome there will be a thousand good things, and most of those are also going to be unintended consequences."

Jesse had noticed in their many phone conversations that Leena had a special way of saying the right thing at the right time. It was as though, when the camera was on her, she could pose the perfect question and was ever eager to put the spotlight back on the other person. It had to be a skill she learned from being a reporter. He had observed people silently from the safety of the shadows for years and concluded that she was not acting. She really wasn't ego-driven, just a good and caring person.

The traffic snarled and became very heavy as they approached another faceless interstate town.

He gave out a small sigh, and asked, "How is it you're still single?"

"You're asking why I'm not married?"

"Uh, yeah."

"Everybody usually asks that question within the first five minutes of meeting me. We've spoken on the phone dozens of times. Why haven't you asked me before? You've thought about it, haven't you?"

"Yeah, I have, but I just assumed if you wanted me to know you would've told me. I guess I'm not a real prying-type person."

"Or just maybe it's because then you'd have to give up some of your own past?"

"I do have a storied past, some good, some bad, probably a lot like you. But truly, I...well, I've thought about why a beautiful woman, like you,"—that brought a quick smile—"is still single."

"What, you think I'm gay?"

"No. No!" He squirmed in his seat.

"I had a man I was interested in…Uh, no, in love with, once," she said slowly. "After that ended, I—"

"You dumped him?"

She nodded.

"Why? No, wait. You don't have to answer that," he said, seeing her frown. "I just assumed that you chose to marry a career instead."

"It's okay. When the two of us didn't work out,"—she let out a small, almost inaudible sigh—"I was fine marrying my job. Most people don't understand that, and would like me to live my life within their parameters. Marriage, kids. There've been countless friends and colleagues who've tried to get me married off, as if I'm not capable of finding a man on my own." She looked at Jesse, a quiet appraisal. "I think it would make them more comfortable if I married."

"You've chosen to be a dead-ender?"

"A what? Dead-ender? Donald Rumsfeld used that term to call Iraqi Ba'ath party members in from the cold during the war. He said they had nowhere to go and hide."

"Yeah, I know. He stole my words. But that's not what it means."

"So, what do your words mean?"

"Each of us is here on earth only because of the people, or more like relatives, that survived wars, famines, and probably hundreds of close calls, which allowed each of us to be born. Actually, you're fifty percent your mom and fifty percent your dad. To take it further. Twenty-five percent your grandfather on your mom's side and so on until at the seventh generation you're less than three-fourths of one percent of everyone." He glanced at her to see if she was getting it. "So, since you and I don't have any children, we effectively kill our entire lineage. We're dead-enders."

"So you're saying that since we have no children, we're killing our own as well as our moms' and dads' future lives? How did you come up with that? Are you really that deep?"

"Do you honestly want to know?"

"Absolutely."

"Okay," he said, taking a deep breath. "Once in a while I read the Bible."

She contemplated him with an eyebrow cocked.

"But don't get me wrong," Jesse said. "I'm not like a biblical scholar or anything and this is not going to be a sermon. I can't quote chapter and verse. But anyway, I was thinking about mortality, and I remembered the Bible said something about seven generations. Look I'm paraphrasing here, okay?"

She nodded.

"If you committed a sexually deviant sin, like molesting a kid, you'd pass the same perversion to the next seven generations. All generations would suffer because of the same sin. At first, I thought that was terribly unfair. Why punish the unborn? Then I wondered why the number seven? So I started to do the math. I understand that geneticists see it differently today, but this is just simple math, and the basic principle is the same today as it was a couple of thousand years ago. Your DNA would essentially not have much influence on that human any more in the seventh generation, since it would be less than one percent. In fact, that particular DNA would have pretty much faded out of existence. That's when I thought how queer it would be not to want to keep on existing."

Once again, Leena glanced over at Jesse.

"Oops, I strayed a little bit. However," he continued, "my point is if you don't have any children, you physically do cease to exist. That's when I developed the term *dead-ender*, and I've used it ever since."

"But I didn't choose not to exist any longer. I just wanted to have a career rather than be a housewife and mom. I thought I'd get around to having a family. It just didn't work out. But you knew you were committing soul suicide, and you didn't do anything about it. Why is that?"

"I believe that some people are sent to earth to do other things. Sometimes it seems that certain people have to be sacrificed so that others can live."

Hidden Truths

"I need to think some more about this," she said, and once again they settled into silence.

Leena reached for her laptop. Jesse could tell the wheels were spinning relentlessly in her mind like the wheels of the Take-Us that were speeding them down the highway to a fate that was sure to change both of their lives.

Chapter 7

The Heart Hears

Jesse wanted to cover about five hundred miles that first day, trying to finish about six p.m. East Coast time. That would mean stopping somewhere around Toledo, Ohio. He thought that would give a great first impression to Leena, or rather the world, about the capability of the car.

Time drifted by and soon they exited the toll road at the city of Maumee, Ohio. He had never heard of it, but assumed it was named after some Indian tribe.

Leena got out of the car with the camera before Jesse drove into the parking lot of the hotel they'd chosen. He could never figure out the difference between a hotel and a motel when you weren't in a big city. It seemed to him that a motel was some place you took a hooker, as in No-Tell Motel. The place they chose was very nice and had more than one floor, but he still couldn't call it a real hotel.

Leena put the camera on a tripod, and after she filmed him pulling in and parking, she stood with the Take-Us in the background and spoke into the camera for a minute. She pushed a couple of buttons on the back of the camera as he walked up to her.

"What are you doing?"

"This is the portable satellite camera that the network owns. I uploaded what I just filmed and it's downloading into a computer at the network as we speak. This is the first time we've used it in the field. It's supposed to be the latest technology."

"What's the advantage to this system?"

"Over what we had, it's tulips to turnips. The picture clarity and sound are far improved. The real advantage is the ease of editing, not to mention you can film breaking news anywhere in the world and have it on the air in just minutes."

"I thought you already had that capability."

"This is a much cleaner set up. And from a corporate stance, it allows us to go into the field with less manpower." She saw the look on his face. "Hey, big companies are always looking for ways to save a buck."

Jesse looked straight into those big beautiful eyes. Damn, she was a gorgeous woman. "You make it easy to forget that you're a big corporate mucky-muck."

"That's a major part of our plan to enslave the masses without them even being aware it's being done," she said with a devilish smile. "But before I can begin implementation of the plan to take over the world, I need to know just one thing. When are you going to feed me? We've been driving all day."

"That sounded like a whine, big corporate mama." Jesse stepped back and put his hands up before her laser-beam eyes sliced him in half. "Why don't we check in first? I'd like to clean up a bit before we eat. Can you hang on that long? I really should have taken the time to install the air conditioning in the car before I left California."

It wouldn't be the last time he wished that.

They checked in and selected two separate rooms that had a connecting door. Leena insisted on paying for both with her corporate credit card. "Business expense," she said.

"I've been written off before, but this is the first time as a business expense," he laughed.

"I certainly hope you're worth it." Leena gave him a frank glance, running her eyes over him.

He unlocked the door and walked into his room, paused, and looked at the connecting door between the separate rooms. Deliberately, he unlocked it and left it slightly ajar. Then he threw his overnight bag onto the bed before turning on the television.

Jesse had lived in California for a long time. The humidity in the Midwest was noticeably higher, and he always seemed to be sticky.

He stripped and went into the bathroom to take a quick shower. It was lucky he wrapped the towel around his waist before he came out of the bathroom.

Leena had kicked off her shoes and was half-sitting, half-lying on his bed, wearing a thin, white, sleeveless top and a pair of black short shorts that showed off her comely legs. She gave him an approving look. "You've taken very good care of yourself, Mr. Christenson. No fat on those bones. Must be all the running you do."

"You certainly don't miss much, do you?" he commented, trying not to stare at the hard, dark circles that were starting to appear through her top.

She patted the coverlet on the bed. "My mom told me about you for many years, and I've had my eye on you for a few long months now, wishing and dreaming I could be with you." She gestured at the front of the towel wrapped around his waist. "I think maybe you now have your eye on me as well."

Jesse sat down on the edge of the bed, hoping the change in posture would help conceal the lump growing beneath his towel. "Leena," he said slowly and half-heartedly. "I'm not into one-night stands any longer. It has to mean more than that."

"I have never been a one-night-stand in my entire life. Search your heart. I think you know me better than that." When she sat up her legs spread apart, and she took his face in both her hands. Her lips were soft and when she opened her mouth and gently put her tongue in his mouth, the taste of her was a sensation he'd forgotten ever existed. Jesse responded, slowly, but it wasn't long before the old became passionately new. The darting of their tongues became a sword match, a thrust and parry created by a single part of each that made the other feel completely whole.

Jesse thought about the many love stories that have been written about first kisses, but none could describe the timelessness and sheer depth of this moment. Time simply didn't exist anymore. It just went on and on. The depth of the kiss was like submerging his face into a clear mountain pool, but somehow still being able to breathe. Somewhere along the way, he became aware of the other parts of his body. His hand was under her shirt, making small, slow circles on top of her flat stomach and steadily moving up. Their breathing was getting more and more ragged, and he finally broke away to take a deep, husky breath. The smell of her perfume burst into his soul. His hand, seeming to have a mind of its own, had reached the base of her breast and he took the time to push her shirt up.

Her breasts were magnificent and abundant, with nipples very dark on her tanned skin. She had beautiful, small nipples, teased into hard little points. He continued to drink in the smell of her perfume. She started to make soft cooing noises, getting louder and louder as he fastened his lips on one of her nipples and started sucking softly. It didn't seem possible, but her nipple got even more tight and hard.

In the meantime, Leena's small hands were not idle. She reached down and ran her hand across his stomach. She unfastened his towel and was beginning to touch—

"This is Leena Delaney, 'On the Road'…"

They both heard Leena's voice and sat up with a start. The television was tuned to WCN and they saw the Take-Us stopping in front of Leena's New York City office.

"I thought we were going to wait to show that," Jesse said, trying to settle his urges down.

"It's not supposed to air until next week," she said in a low, sexy voice, still breathing hard. On the television, she was just getting into the car. Leena jumped off the bed, pulling her shirt down and covering those perfect breasts. "I've got to find out what's going on," she said as she walked into the adjoining room.

Jesse stood up and got off the bed. The towel fell to the floor. Looking down, he wondered if blue balls really did exist and if his were going to fall off. He was in the process of putting on his underwear when Leena came back into the room with a cell phone to her ear. She was listening as she looked at him, smiling and mouthing the words, *nice butt.*

"I understand that, but who authorized it?" Leena walked in circles, one hand twirling her hair. "He did?" Her eyebrows shot up. "I forgot to turn my phone back on after we did the last shot.

But still, you should have waited and…" She kept talking as she walked back into the other room.

Jesse watched the TV segment for the next few minutes as he got dressed. He had to admit that he did come off as an expert of sorts. The shot of him opening the hood and showing a bank of batteries with no motor was very impressive.

"That was our own Leena Delaney, who's riding shotgun. We'll continue checking in over the next few days as the Take-Us-mobile continues its incredible journey to San Francisco," the anchor said. "Next up, the greatest story never told. 'Have we already won the War on Terror?' Stick around; we'll be right back after this word from our sponsors."

Jesse had just finished tying his shoes when Leena walked in and said, "I blew it."

He noticed she had changed into a short skirt and put on a different top and, sadly, a bra. "What happened?"

"Just bad luck, really. After the last shot I forgot to turn my cell phone back on."

"I thought *you* made the decision of what stories got put on and when."

"I do, but since I'm gone this week, my boss, Donald Eugene, is doing my job, though that's not the real problem. The real boss, the owner of the network, was visiting the office today…you know who that is, don't you? Anyway, Donald was demonstrating the benefits and flexibility of the new camera I showed you. The boss saw the story and insisted we air it right away. Donald tried to call me, but it wouldn't have made any difference. You don't just say no to the owner."

Jesse shrugged. "What's done is done. We can't take back those words or scenes even if we wanted to. Let's go get some dinner, and we can talk about what we should do next."

Leena came over to him with a saucy step and put both arms around his neck. "I know that. It's just the timing that sucked. We'll just have to continue this after dinner. It will be even better then." She gave him a warm kiss as he pulled her close. She broke off the kiss and whispered, "I can hardly wait."

Jesse felt the same way. "We could just stay here…but then we'd miss dinner…but we'd have the rest of the night without any distractions. God, I'm wishy-washy as hell." He slowly stepped out of the embrace. "All right, after dinner."

The hotel had a nice restaurant. When they finally got to the hostess after waiting in line, she told them it would be a twenty minutes and asked if they would like to wait in the bar. He looked at Leena, she nodded, and they headed off in that direction.

There were two empty bar stools in the crowded room. They sat down. An older man in a worn sports jacket sitting next to Jesse leaned over and checked out Leena. The man then looked at him, tilting his head questioningly then resumed looking straight ahead at the mirror in front of him. The bartender waddled over and took their order. Jesse decided on a mug of Coors Lite draft beer, and Leena ordered a glass of merlot. Jesse looked at the end of the bar where there was a TV set and, sure enough, WCN was on.

When he looked ahead, he could see the man next to him studying them in the mirror. The man made a movement with his head, as if he'd made some kind of great decision and turned to them. "I just saw you two on the news. That was you, wasn't it?"

Jesse heard Leena mutter under her breath, "And so it begins."

Not knowing what else to say he just said, "Yep, that was us."

"Does it really work like you said?" Catching himself, the man added, "I guess it must. You're here, aren't you? All the way to San Francisco, that's a long haul. Think you'll make it?"

"It does work. What we didn't say in the story is that I already drove it from California to New York, so we know it will easily go that far again."

"Damn, you don't say. Listen, I don't mean to bother you, but my name is Bob Moore." He poked out his stubby hand, which Jesse shook. "I work for General Motors. Hybrid Division. When I saw that story, the what-do-you-call-it—oh, yeah, the Take-Us—I just thought…it's such a simple idea, why didn't anybody else think of it a long time ago?" Bob rambled on, asking many good questions.

It was obvious the fellow had a deep background in this field.

The bartender came over with their drinks. Leena looked over at Jesse, raised her glass in a toast, and said with a coy smile, "To the future. May it arrive tonight."

Jesse clicked his glass with hers, took a deep gulp of cold beer, and wondered how far into the future she was looking. She had such expressive eyes.

Bob also raised his glass.

The three chatted until the hostess finally saved them by telling them their table was ready. They said goodbye to Bob, and this time he shook both their hands. When they parted he said, "May God bless you both." He had his cell phone out and started punching in a number before they turned away.

While they were walking to their table, Jesse whispered over Leena's shoulder, "He sure is an excitable character."

She stopped abruptly and said, "It's going to be very exciting to a whole bunch of people. You do get that, don't you? Your idea has been unleashed."

Dinner was a long, drawn-out affair. It took hours to finish, helped by two bottles of wine. The clean-up crew started to vacuum under their feet, and Jesse's eyes started to slip downward. "So how do you stay in such great shape?" he asked, straining to lift his eyes back to her face.

"When I'm in town I go to the health club and work out with weights three times a week. The other three days I go to school and practice Tae Kwan Do. I'm a third-degree Black Belt, so you should watch your step, buster, or I'll kick your ass."

"Somebody has had too much wine," Jesse said, swirling the red liquid clockwise.

"We'll see." She reached over and touched his hand. "I'll be glad to wrestle with you real soon." Her expression turned serious. "You don't have to tell me, Jesse, but just how many women have you been with since your wife died?" Her eyes narrowed a bit and the way she asked meant he had to answer.

"Um. Just a couple…or a few," he lied.

"So is it a couple or a few?"

"Probably a few."

"And what's the definition of a few? Is it more than one?" she asked, moving her chair closer.

"More than one?"

"Don't act so dumb. You're a rotten liar, Jesse Christenson."

"Is this your reporter persona?" he asked, putting down his wine glass and sitting up straight.

"Stop trying to change the subject."

"I knew I was in trouble when you said my full name."

"There you go again, trying to change the subject. Admit it. You haven't been with a woman since your wife. Have you?"

"Okay, it's true. I haven't. And I'm not trying to change the subject, but you're not getting any more wine."

"I knew it. You don't need to be ashamed of carrying the torch for so many years." She ignored his statement and filled their glasses with the last of the second bottle. "I could tell by the look in your eyes. Hunger and fear mixed," she slurred. "I can tolerate a lot, but not lying. Please don't ever lie to me again or I will do something really horrible to you."

"Like what?"

"I don't know yet." She tilted her head and slammed back the full glass of wine. "I'll think of something. It's a long way to California." She stood up a little wobbly, leaned over, and whispered into his ear. "Take me back to your room so I can screw your eyeballs out."

Two parts of Jesse stood up immediately. Leena took his hand and walked out of the restaurant in the direction of the elevator. Out of the corner of his eye, Jesse saw a gentleman rise out of a chair in the hotel lobby and approach them. As the man drew near, Jesse let go of Leena's hand. The man wore a dark, expensive suit with a red tie and looked extremely successful.

"Are you Mr. Jesse Christenson?" the man asked, appearing a little unsettled.

Jesse nodded, wondering if strangers appearing out of nowhere and knowing his name was how it was going to be from now on.

"I'm sorry to bother you. I know it's late…" Getting no comment from either of them, he continued. "My name is Richard DeMonroe, and I'm the president of the Hybrid Motor Division at General Motors. One of our engineers called me, Bob Moore…I think you met him earlier tonight? He told me you were here."

Jesse glanced around but didn't see Bob. "Yes, we met earlier," he said, hoping he wasn't slurring his words.

"I must say, after that news segment on WCN today, you certainly have rattled the nuts out of the tree." Mr. DeMonroe sounded breathless. "I just drove down from Detroit. It's only about an hour away."

"So does that mean you're one of the nuts?" Jesse asked, wishing he could take it back. He would have to keep in mind that he'd drunk about a bottle of wine.

"I guess so." DeMonroe smiled as if they were old friends sharing a private joke. "Listen, can we talk about your invention?"

Jesse looked at Leena. She looked sloshed. "Why don't you go up to your room, Leena? I'll see you in the morning."

"You boys…always talking business." She shook her head. "Okay, I'll see you in the morning. Nice to meet you, Mr. DeMonroe."

DeMonroe nodded and smiled at her. She got into the elevator and after the door closed, he said, "She's as pretty in real life as she is on television."

"I suppose you didn't drive all the way down here just to check her out."

"No, of course not. I asked the hotel if we could borrow a meeting room for a few minutes, and they agreed. Would it be okay if we spoke there?" All business now, he led the way, opening the door to the hotel's conference room. Jesse could see they weren't going to be alone. There sat old Bob at a large meeting table, along with a smaller, darker man.

"This is Farid, my executive secretary, and you already know Bob."

Bob stood up and offered his hand again, which Jesse ignored. "Gosh, I'm sorry, Mr. Christenson, but I just couldn't help but call my boss and tell him that I met you, right here outside of Toledo.

And I guess he called his boss, who called his—"

"Yeah, I get it. It's cool," Jesse said and flashed him a little smile. Bob relaxed slightly.

"I've spoken to many of our finest engineers in the last hour," DeMonroe said, taking charge. "All of them agree. You might be onto something big. How big?" He shrugged his shoulders. "Nobody seems to know until we can evaluate it more closely."

"Certainly Bob must have told you the car has been from California to New York and back to here. Plus it had a whole lot of test miles before that. And you think I *might* be onto something big? No wonder the Japanese are kickin' the shit out of your business."

"Point taken. Okay, I'm not one to beat around the bush, so let me just ask you straight up. What do you intend to do with your invention? Surely you don't intend to go into business against us, do you?"

Instead of answering the question, Jesse asked one of his own. "What would you, or rather your corporation, do with the car if you owned it?"

"If it proved to be the great idea it seems to be, and if it was economically feasible, we would mass produce it, of course. Selling cars is how we make our money, you know."

"Let's see now, you'd buy the patent from me, and then you'd have to get rid of all the parts and inventory you've already manufactured for all the cars you're currently building. That could take years."

"It takes a battleship a lot of room and time to turn around," DeMonroe said.

"I bet like hell it could turn much faster if another battleship came up on it and started firing," Jesse said, raising his voice. "Your corporation would of course have a monopoly because you're rich and powerful enough to defend yourself anywhere in the world. My worry is that you'd shelve the Take-Us for years or maybe forever."

The room was as silent as the depths of space for a few long seconds. "I came down here not as a threat, but to offer you a legitimate business proposal. If we do consummate a deal, there is no way for me to guarantee if your invention would ever go into production…or when."

"You've been the first to speak to me about the Take-Us," Jesse said, standing up. "And I would like to thank you for not bullshitting me. In order to educate the country and promote my idea, I have to finish the drive to San Francisco—not to mention I promised myself, and all that I consider holy, that I would do so. I'll get back in touch with you shortly. Maybe we can work out some kind of deal. Is that fair?" he asked, reaching out his hand.

"Yes," Mr. DeMonroe said, taking his hand, "but can I ask one small favor?"

"What would that be?"

"How about you take Bob, Farid, and me for a ride?"

Jesse looked over at Bob, who looked like a dog in heat with his tongue hanging out. You just had to love car people. "Why not? What can it hurt?"

DeMonroe sat up front and Bob and Farid sat in the back. "I see you have a tiger for luck," Farid said with a thick accent as he took the tiger out of the back window, putting it on his lap. "It is very good luck."

"Yeah, it came with the car," Jesse said.

"Let's see what this baby can do," Bob said, sounding like a teenager.

Jesse gave them a short ride, taking it up to a hundred on a deserted highway. That brought an "Ah" from the back seat. Even the president of GM's Hybrid Motor Division seemed impressed. When Jesse returned them to the hotel parking lot, they all thanked him, pumping his hand. DeMonroe gave Jesse his business card and made him promise to call.

Jesse slid his finger onto the button when he entered the elevator. He smiled in anticipation. He had not forgotten what was waiting for him upstairs in the hotel room.

He unlocked and opened the door to the room and saw Leena pacing back and forth. She had changed out of her short skirt and had jeans on. "Come on, we have got to get out of here," she said, reaching down and picking up his bag.

Jesse took his bag from her hand and saw she had repacked it. "What's happening?"

Leena was stone-cold sober. "Think about it. If they could find us that easily, who else would want to find us as quickly as possible? We're only a short drive from Dearborn, Michigan, home of the largest Islamic population in America. I didn't think this would begin so quickly."

He picked up on Leena's fear. "I know a safe place, and it's not that far away. You remember I grew up in Indiana, right?" Leena nodded and he continued. "I know a good place to hide out. We'll be safe there."

They sneaked out of the hotel and got into the Take-Us, slipping out of the parking lot with no lights on. They were on the toll road in a short time and tried their best to watch the road behind them to see if they were being followed. It was pretty dead this late at night. Jesse believed they'd gotten away clean.

He pried his eyes off the mirror he kept studying as if their lives depended on it. "What do you think?"

"I don't think we're being followed." She was also watching intently, half turned in her seat.

Jesse drove fast, hoping his too-much-wine headache would go away. His mind rumbled. He looked at Leena and said, "I wonder who else watched that segment."

Chapter 8

Evil Awakens

The time difference was almost eight and a half hours between Tehran and the Take-Us.

Colonel Teymour Mafsanjani stepped briskly out of the elevator, a cloud of smoke surrounding him. He was accompanied by Lieutenant Mustafa Kourani, a newly commissioned junior officer who came from a fine family, his brother the current head of Hezbollah's security division in Lebanon. The two passed several door openings before they entered a well-equipped interrogation room that resembled a surgical suite.

Mafsanjani was anxious and a little excited about speaking to the female American spy they'd arrested the night before. He saw that she was sitting naked and upright in the specially designed chair. Her arms and legs were strapped tightly to their respective supports. The golden hair that had covered her head was for the most part hacked off. Only a few stubbles remained. The woman's head was hanging down, chin on her chest. Alligator clips connected the electrical wires pinched firmly to the tips of her light-brown nipples. The dried blood and burn marks were indicative of too much voltage. Bruises covered her pallid body, and blood had oozed out of her, crusted now on the only hair she had left.

"Turn off that machine," Mafsanjani ordered, turning to the young lieutenant.

Mustafa Kourani turned to the big, slovenly man with the small, stupid eyes who was operating the machine and made a frantic signal to stop what he was doing. The big man turned a knob and the hum that filled the room stopped.

Mafsanjani took the captive's chin in one hand, lifted up her head and looked into her empty, sightless eyes. He crushed the cigarette he was holding with his other hand into the center of her forehead.

"She is dead." Mafsanjani looked at the big man. "How much did we get out of her?"

The slovenly man just shrugged his shoulders and said indifferently, "She never spoke."

Mafsanjani turned furiously to Kourani. "Did you not just bring her in here?"

"It was only ten, maybe fifteen minutes ago, Colonel, s-s-sir. I stepped out to meet you at the elevator. She must have had a bad heart," said the suddenly pale and anxious young officer.

"Did all the men on duty enjoy her charms throughout the night?"

"Sir, it's a matter of custom for the men to take their pleasure with the infidel whores before we start questioning," the lieutenant stammered.

"How did she act when you brought her in? Scared, weeping, struggling? What was her demeanor?" Mafsanjani shouted to the slovenly man.

The big man once again shrugged his shoulders. "We had to drag her in. She was barely awake." He pointed to the tops of her feet, from which the skin had been scraped off, blood visible.

"Of course she was out of it. She was drugged! Someone got to her! How long have you been here? I do not remember seeing you before." Colonel Mafsanjani squinted at the big man with the stupid eyes. "Open your mouth!"

The big man just stared, unmoving. Then he frowned, his animal instincts aroused. The colonel reached down and took his nine-millimeter pistol—a Smith and Wesson he'd confiscated from an American spy—out of the shoulder holster he always wore under his jacket. "I order you to open your mouth!"

This time the big man complied, but his eyes had narrowed and were full of fear. Colonel Mafsanjani jammed the pistol into his open mouth. "She was worth more to me alive than you are."

The colonel squeezed the trigger, and the pistol slammed one slug deep into the lout's throat. Mafsanjani watched, detached, as the man's brains splattered over the rear wall and the body sank to the floor and lay still, like a pile of rotten garbage. The colonel turned to Kourani, who was pale and shaking.

"S–S-Sir, it is the quality of men we now have to use. All our best interrogators are in Iraq. We just do n-n-not have enough experienced men left. The Americans are killing them all."

Colonel Mafsanjani slowly put the pistol away. He reached into his jacket, removed a pack he shook absently, and lit another cigarette. "You would be wise to keep that particular opinion to yourself."

Kourani nodded, too frightened to say more. The colonel calmly continued. "We who are in the intelligence branch know secrets that few others dare dream of. That is why even these routine interrogations must be handled very delicately."

"Yes, sir," Kourani said, his voice returning. Some of the color was coming back into his face now that he realized he wasn't going to be executed.

"Get this mess cleaned up and make sure your men know what happened to that big piece of shit." Mafsanjani gestured at the dead man. "It never hurts to have your men fear you. You will be surprised at how much harder they will try to please you." A sinister smile touched his lips. "Have the woman's body taken in for a blood screen. I want to know what type of poison she was given."

"How do you know she was poisoned?" Kourani looked at the colonel's face and added, "Sir."

"When you've done this as many times as I have, you've seen everything. It was probably Persantine or something similar that speeds her heart up, so when we touch her with electricity here"—he pointed to her left breast—"her heart literally explodes."

"But, sir, why not a complete autopsy?"

"Just her blood. I already know how she died." He shook his head. "She would have been executed later, regardless, but we wanted her secrets first. The Americans always believe they can send newswomen over here and that we will not be suspicious. Remember this, Kourani. The prettier the woman, the more likely she is a spy."

"Yes, sir. What should I do with the body?"

"As always, take it back to Iraq. Do not forget to behead her first. In fact, do it immediately."

The colonel headed back to the elevator and used his special key to open the elevator door. It was the only elevator that accessed the interrogation level that was located three stories below the street, and few keys were issued. Every shift change a duty officer would escort the replacement crew down and check the outgoing crew for proper and complete identification. There had never been an escape from the third level. If there were an escape, the duty officer would be executed, right after he tasted the bitter fare from level three. Every duty officer knew this, which is probably why the system worked so well.

Mafsanjani stepped out of the special elevator, walked casually to the main, unsecured elevator, which would take him to his office on the sixth floor. There were many men present, appearing as if they were just casually hanging around the lobby. He did not allow any of his men to wear their uniforms to work or have any weapons in sight.

One of the first things he had done on becoming the commander of the state counter-intelligence service VEVAK, an independent service of the larger and more internally focused SAVAMA, was to move certain essential parts of the group out of the large military complex nearby. He was sure the Americans had it targeted; he had seen the information himself. Moving into this nondescript building on the outskirts of the city was much wiser. Some thought he was too paranoid, but that was his job, to always be paranoid. He knew, even if some had forgotten, that when his country had declared war on America almost thirty years before, it would just be a matter of time until the Great Satan came calling.

When he entered his outer office, one of his assistants got up from his desk, and came over to greet him. "Colonel Mafsanjani, President Ahmadinejad called and demanded that you call immediately upon returning from down below."

The colonel ran his fingers through his black hair. He had been expecting this. "Get the rabid Little Nib on the phone for me."

The staff knew of the animosity between the two leaders, but Mafsanjani put his fingers to his lips as if the name-calling were a state secret, although the general populace also called the president the Little Nib.

Mafsanjani unlocked and walked into his office, turning on the filtering machine that would scan for listening devices that may have been planted since his departure just thirty minutes ago. He arranged himself behind the desk, reached forward, and turned the smiling picture of his forever-young wife a few degrees to the left just as the phone buzzed. He thought the Little Nib must have had the phone up his ass, awaiting his call.

"Colonel Mafsanjani," the president began in a snide, formal tone, "I have been on the phone with many oil ministers from OPEC." His voice turned challenging and he screamed, "Have you not heard of this…this…Take-Us automobile?"

"Yes, Your Excellency. I learned about it several hours ago."

"Then why didn't you tell me about it immediately? This man Christenson, he is a Jew?"

"Excellency, if you would check over your correspondence, you would see that I sent a special communiqué…hours ago." Then just to placate the Little Nib, Mafsanjani added, "He probably is a Jew."

"Just as I thought. They called me at the Presidential Residence and when I came to my office, the phone! It will not stop ringing! I've been talking nonstop since then—" The president rustled papers and slapped his desk. "Ah, there it is. You do recognize the significance of this, don't you?"

"All too well, Your Excellency." Mafsanjani wondered when the *palace* became the *Presidential Residence.*

"OPEC has authorized one hundred million dollars to buy this-this-this—what's it called again?"

"I believe it's called the Take-Us automobile." The colonel ground out his cigarette in an ashtray made from a human skull. It scared the crap out of his subordinates.

"Yes, that's it. What have you found out about it?"

"Your Excellency, as you know, it is still night in America and our contacts have not yet arrived at their offices. The way their Homeland Security operates is that if we do anything out of the ordinary, they will figure out that we are up to something. I have put out emails to some of our sleeper cells asking for information. As yet, I have not received anything in return."

"I don't care what they figure. This is the worst threat our country has ever faced. Why did the Americans put this on the TV? Are they trying to provoke us into attacking?"

"Your Excellency, I have explained this many times." Mafsanjani took a sip of his cold coffee. "The West does not block information as we do. The network probably just hit on this story and tried to beat the competition to it."

"I am ordering you to eliminate this threat. Use anything or anyone, spend whatever it takes. If you do not succeed, the greatest asset of our country—" He stopped abruptly, trying to gain control. His next sentence was less shrill. "The price of oil will plummet and we will be ruined. The only bargaining chip we have will disappear, just like our dreams of a nuclear program."

"Your Excellency, I have foreseen all of that and more, and I would suppose most of the other oil producers in the world see it, too. That would also include the United States, the third largest oil producer in the world."

"I don't care about the Great Satan. You get this fixed or your ass will be mine."

"Your Excellency, I have always faithfully served our country and Allah—may peace be upon him—which are the same."

"Praise Allah if you wish, Colonel, but do not fail me."

Mafsanjani put the phone down slowly, lit another cigarette, and thought about the options. If the American called Christenson took the hundred million dollars that OPEC put up, then the Iranians would put together a disinformation program to prove the theory was science-fiction junk. It would be readied to go immediately. If the American did not take the money, he would be kidnapped and forced to sign away his rights. Then he would have an unpleasant accident…perhaps the car would blow up. That would be easy to put into motion. Whatever happened, the colonel could not allow that auto to get to San Francisco.

He started an e-mail.

Day Two

Chapter 9

DHS—The First Sniff

Patrick O'Hallohan looked at his watch: three a.m. The night before around this time, he'd been with that blond congressional intern, Melissa. The drunker he got, the more he kept calling her Monica, until she finally faced him and asked if he was trying to give her a hint. He'd woken up alone, with a nasty hangover.

O'Hallohan spotted Richard Gustoffson, the Deputy Director in charge of Domestic Terrorism Operations for the Department of Homeland Security. He was on the far side of the large situation room, which was patterned after the NASA flight control room. O'Hallohan wondered when the last time was that Gustoffson had come to work at three o'clock in the morning.

The other higher-ups had not yet arrived.

O'Hallohan began to make his way to Gustoffson, who had stopped and was looking up at the large, liquid-crystal map of the world, lights blinking to highlight potential problem areas in the continental United States.

O'Hallohan walked briskly up and stood silently next to the DD, waiting for Gustoffson to finish reading the ticker running under the map.

"What's going on?" Gustoffson asked. "This better be good. I didn't get to bed until after midnight. The friggin' Yankees blew it again in the twelfth inning." Looking up at O'Hallohan's face and unkempt red hair, he continued. "What are you doing here, anyway?"

A former Army Delta Force captain, O'Hallohan spent most of his time in the field. "Filling in for Sanchez. He's on vacation until this weekend. It wasn't my choice," said temporary Night Duty Officer O'Hallohan.

"It's good for you to come in from the field every once in awhile," the DD said with a tired smile. "So what do we have here?" He pointed at the huge map on the wall.

"Sir, we've never seen this much open communication from the entire suspected and known terrorist network locations. The duty staff and I agree that we have a terrorist event of some type about to happen,"

"What type of event?" Gustoffson asked, his short-lived smile disappearing.

"Like always at the beginning, we don't know yet, but—and this is a big but—we've also picked up traffic from most of the sovereign oil-producing countries that we suspect of providing terrorist support."

"I guess by that you mean Iran and the Saudis?"

"Yes sir, but also all the other Middle Eastern OPEC countries, and Mexico, and Venezuela. There's even chatter coming from Russia and, as weird as it may sound, China."

"China? They don't have any oil to speak of. Just huge buyers."

"That's why we called you in, sir. Something is definitely out of sorts."

"Has there been any type of increased military activity from any of them?"

"The CIA and Pentagon report that everything appears to be pretty much normal."

"So what's happened that's stirred up this hornet's nest? Could this be some kind of coordinated financial attack?"

"We've checked the financial markets. There's no news or disaster that may have changed the price of oil. It's trading slightly higher than yesterday, but less than a percent on the international markets. About normal."

"I'll alert the Secretary. We must presume that a terrorist attack is coming. Get me the pertinent information, and when the rest of the senior staff arrives, call me. We'll meet in the conference room. Incidentally, where is the President?"

"At the White House tonight."

"Good work, so far. Keep digging. Act like they're coming after your house."

"They are, sir."

"Hmm, interesting thought. How about a hot cup of coffee, and let's try to get this thing figured out. If it's as bad as it seems to be, get everybody prepared to go to Threat Level Red."

"Let them know that we know?"

"It's worked before as a preventative. Maybe they'll think we actually do know something."

Chapter 10

The Aged Barn

Leena breathed softly, sound asleep, her face smashed up against the window glass. Every time she exhaled, a tiny bit of fog would appear under her nose. It would have been funny, but he'd been driving for three hours and his wine-buzz was fading. He had started to tire. It was past three o'clock in the morning. He'd kept an eye on the rearview mirror, but he knew there could have been an entire convoy of cops, or enemies, and he wouldn't have been able pick them out from any of the other cars on the toll road.

Jesse's hasty plan, conceived with a blood alcohol level above the legal limit, was to get off at the exit for Mishawaka, Indiana, named after an Indian princess. He knew it well. He'd grown up there. It had been more than thirty years since the last time he'd set foot in his hometown. He had no relatives living there anymore; all had died or moved away years ago. The house he'd grown up in was out in the country. His family had only owned a couple of acres, but there had been several large farms nearby. He was hoping some of the old barns, which were mostly deserted, had not fallen down yet.

Sparks danced between forgotten memories in his mind as he drove up the lane between the hedgerows. His vision was getting blurry, but he could still see by his headlights that the lane had seen some traffic recently. He assumed it was from the tractors the farmers used to plow the adjacent fields.

He drove into a deserted barn and turned out the lights. It was morbidly dark, and he was bone-tired. Leena was sleeping peacefully. He leaned against his door and had barely closed his eyes when the morning sunlight, shining through the gaps in the roof, blasted holes through his eyelids.

"Good morning," Leena said, watching him. "You snore."

"Good morning to you, too. I don't snore. I just breathe loud," he said, still groggy.

"So you're one of those crabby ones, aren't you? I didn't mean to insult you. I was just going to tell you that I found your snoring very comforting, knowing that you were so much at peace."

"What a diplomat," he said, seeing her smile. "Sorry, I didn't mean to bite. I need a cup of java."

"Apology accepted. I would be glad to get you a cup of coffee, but…" She waved her hand toward the windshield. "Just where are we, anyway?"

"Indiana. I grew up about a half mile from here."

"I don't suppose there's a bathroom around?"

"Well, not really. We can go back into town. It's only about fifteen or twenty minutes away."

"I'm a country girl," she said, reaching for the door handle. "I'll just find me a quiet corner somewhere."

Leena got out of the car and disappeared around a corner of the barn. Jesse reached into the blue Igloo cooler on the back seat for a bottle of water. He had a bad case of dragon-mouth this morning. He got out of the car and stretched his back that was tied into knots from sleeping in the front seat of the car. He tried to remember… how much wine did he drink?

"I'll have a drink of that, if you don't mind," Leena said, walking silently up behind him.

He turned quickly. "Damn, you scared the bejesus out of me! Drink. Sure, no problem." She snickered and he ignored it. "How can you look so good this morning?"

"You're sweet." She took a swallow of water and then gave him a quick kiss. "I haven't forgotten last night. But I was thinking that maybe we should shoot today's progress report right here in the barn. It would be a great backdrop, and there's no way anybody watching would ever be able to figure out exactly where we are.

Right?" She turned and looked around in the barn. "Where did all these old signs come from?"

"They were always here, from the time I was a kid." He looked at the signs mounted onto the faded natural wood planks that made up the sides of the old barn. There were many. One was City Service, another Gulf Oil, and still another Sun Oil Company. "They're probably the only thing holding up the walls in this place."

"It would be a great contrast to our story. It's very private in here."

"Do you really think we need to be so careful this soon?"

"It doesn't seem so pressing in the light of the morning. Even so, last night in the solitude of the hotel room I had this bad feeling. I still feel something isn't quite right." She surveyed the interior of the barn.

"Woman's intuition? The more I think of it, it seems we should be all right for another few days. They couldn't organize that fast, could they?"

"Just because you're an optimist, doesn't change the truth. Don't dismiss me so easily."

"I'm sorry, I—"

"Look, last year Exxon had about four hundred billion dollars of income. Stop and think about how many actual countries made even more than that through the oil business. Now tell me how fast you'd move to protect that. If only—"

It was Jesse's turn to interrupt. "Listen, it's not your fault the network broadcast the story early. That's probably what you feel." She shook her head. "Believe me, there are forces at work here that are much greater than the two of us."

"Yeah, you're probably right," she said, with a beautiful smile reappearing like the sun from behind a cloud. "I guess it's been done, and it is what it is. Too late to take it back. Let's get this next segment shot and get back on the road."

He bent down to look at himself in the side mirror when he heard her laugh behind him. "Come on, open the trunk. Or is it still the hood?" She wrinkled her nose. "We'll just put a hat on you and maybe with a lick and promise get you presentable for the camera."

Leena set up the camera on the tripod and then went to the same exterior mirror, touched up her make-up, put a WCN cap on, and pulled her shoulder-length hair through the hole in the back of the cap. When she saw him watching, she said, "This is a trade secret. If you ever see those girl reporters on TV with a hat on it's because they didn't have time to do their hair."

She got the camera rolling, a term that doesn't really translate in a digital world. Sometimes it just takes time for the words to catch up with technology.

"Good morning. This is Leena Delaney, 'On the Road' with the fantastic Take-Us automobile. Yesterday we left New York City. We had a very enjoyable ride of approximately seven hundred miles without any stops for gas, though we did stop for food and those little inconveniences that plague all travelers," she said with a shy smile. "I can attest that the Take-Us is a very smooth and, so far, dependable automobile."

Jesse took over and worked the camera which was mounted on a tripod as Leena walked to the car.

"As you can see," Leena said as she raised her hand to gesture to the inside of the barn, "we are filming from the inside of an abandoned barn."

Jesse panned slowly as she indicated he should do, picking up most of the old signs. Then he put Leena square in the middle of the crosshairs on the camera lens. She gestured for him to join her.

"Mr. Christenson, yesterday you were telling me just how this car would change America. Could you now please tell the viewers what you described to me?"

"Yes, of course. This auto has so many potential benefits it's difficult to explain them all in one sitting. This is not necessarily in the order of importance." He put up one finger. "The first thing is how it would open up our country to families who, because of the cost of gasoline, can't afford to travel anymore. Imagine if you would, the only things folks would have to pack is some food and maybe a tent. They could travel for no cost throughout this fabulous country. When I speak of no cost, I mean not having to pay for gas, which has doubled in price over the last few years. The experts are claiming it will go over twelve dollars a gallon in the near future. Many people will of course want to stay in motels, which would bring a boom to that market again, along with the thousands of restaurants along the way. Some people might not choose to travel, but they commute to work every day. I'd be willing to bet most don't subtract from their wages how much they spend on fuel a month. That money savings could go directly into their pockets."

"So most people would save money, some maybe thousands of dollars a year?"

"Yes, but it's more than just saving money. It's a matter of giving people more control of their own destinies. When Americans travel through the different states, they discover it's not a red state versus blue contest anymore. Traveling allows us all to mix and see that we're not so different. I don't really know how to say this, but we've been at war since 9/11. It just doesn't feel like it because none of us have had to suffer like our relatives did back in World War II, unless of course you're one of those who have volunteered to take your turn and serve our country to protect the rest of us. I know that many of you would be more willing to help if it were possible. But how? Right now, every time you fill up your gas tank, a portion of your money ends up in the hands of the Islamic jihadists we're fighting. Our country could step totally out of that conflict if we were not so dependent on foreign oil. This car only uses, at most, a couple of quarts of oil per year."

"That certainly is a compelling reason for the development of your car," Leena said. "You have others?"

"Just think, a few short years from now Los Angeles and cities in similar situations would have beautiful blue skies with no smog problems. Many of the associated health problems would decrease or go away altogether. Look, I'm not saying this car is the answer to all the world's problems, but it is a solution to one of the biggies right now."

"We will have more of this interview tomorrow when we continue to report 'On the Road' with the Take-Us," Leena said, as she signed off.

"How do you think that went?" Jesse asked. "Too much horse-shit?"

"No. Not at all. I think the viewers will see you as a concerned deep-thinker and one who's a hopeless optimist." Leena laughed as she pushed the transmit button. "Whoops, there's a red light. I think I have to take this outside where it has a clear view of the sky so it can find a satellite." She picked up the camera and went out the back door of the barn.

Jesse put the tripod in the trunk and rearranged all the other gear they had haphazardly thrown into the back seat the night before.

"Turn around, very slow, and poot your hands up."

Jesse spun and crouched at the same time, but after seeing the black semi-automatic pistol pointed at his chest, he stood up straight and put his hands in the air. "Listen, mister. I don't want any trouble. I was just leaving your barn."

"Where ees girl?"

"What girl? She's gone. I left her back in Ohio." He took a step to his right to put the car between the two of them.

"Stand steell. I heard you talking a minute ago."

"Who are you?"

"I'm your enemy, infidel," the man said, a vicious grin crossing his face. "Where ees girl?" The man waved the gun away and then centered it on Jesse's chest.

Jesse knew exactly where Leena was: twenty feet behind the man and closing fast. He looked directly at his captor, so his eyes wouldn't give her away.

Jesse raised his voice to mask any noise Leena might make. "If I'm your enemy, then you know you're nothing to me but a stinking pig. I would never give my woman up to a pig like you. Go fuck yourself!"

"It weel be a pleasure to keel you, but not yet. They said bring you in alife, but they didn't say I could not shoot you." The man lowered the gun sight to Jesse's legs.

He wasn't a big man, only about five foot six. Leena hit him on his gun arm with the side of her hand. A karate chop, Jesse thought. The gun boomed and the bullet flew harmlessly into the packed dirt floor. The pistol fell out of the man's fingers and landed on the barn floor.

"You beetch! You broke it," the man screamed, holding his arm.

Jesse moved fast and punched the guy in the center of the face. The man went down hard and lay sprawled on his back. Leena calmly reached down and picked up his gun.

Jesse kicked the man in the side of his jaw. "Don't you *ever* point a gun at me."

The man's eyes closed like the lights going out in a bar after last call. Jesse started to walk away, but was so pissed he stalked back and kicked the man straight in the balls. "And *that's* for calling my gal a bitch!"

"You know he's unconscious and doesn't feel a thing."

"I guarantee he will when he wakes up," Jesse shouted, adrenaline pouring through his veins. "Why are you sticking up for him, anyhow?"

"Sticking up for him? I wouldn't piss up his ass if his stomach was on fire."

"What?"

"It's something my girlfriend's granddad used to say." A slight blush crept into Leena's face. "But that's not what I meant about him being unconscious. We needed to find out if he's alone or if there are more of them out there." She gestured toward the front door the gunman had just come in. "You kind of took that option off the table."

"Oh shit, I forgot about that." Jesse ran to the car and pulled out his own pistol from the overnight bag, a .22 Colt Automatic Match Target. It only held ten rounds, not exactly a combat weapon. He pulled the safety back and was ready to shoot. He'd learned long ago that only dead men carried unloaded guns. He ran to the front door and noticed that Leena had gone to the rear. After thirty seconds, he yelled, "I don't see anyone. I don't even see the car he came in."

Leena walked back to the unconscious man and said, "Nobody

back there, either."

"The brush is so thick out along the lane an army could be hiding out there and we'd never see them. Come on, we need to get out of here."

"What about him?" she asked, looking down and studying the man.

"I'm on it." He ran to the hood, which was now serving as the trunk of the car. "I have some wire ties in my toolbox." He opened the toolbox; the ties were on top. He moved back to the man, put the plastic wire ties around his wrists, and zipped them together behind his back. He did the same to the man's ankles. Leena searched through the man's pockets.

"I guess we could use the cell phone to call the police," Jesse said. "But then we'd have to stick around and answer a lot of questions."

"Jesse, we have a real problem." Leena stood up and held out a sheriff's badge. "He *is* the police…"

"Wait a minute. You heard what he said."

"I heard."

"He was going to shoot me in the leg."

"I saw him."

"He said he was going to kill me."

"I heard that, too."

"Shit. Is he a cop or not?"

"I don't know. Maybe he was just trying to scare us."

"Look at him. He's dark-complexioned. He looks Arab. And remember when he spoke to me? He had an accent."

"He could be a Mexican, or some other Hispanic culture."

"Wait, he called me an infidel. No real sheriff would say that, would he?" Unsure now, Jesse walked to the front door and surveyed the lane again.

"We can't stay here and keep debating this. We'll have to call the real sheriff when we get someplace safe. And if this guy is the real thing," she said, shaking her head, "I'll have to call my boss and have him post bail if no one believes our story. I don't see anything out there, do you?"

"No, the brush is just too thick."

"We need to go."

"All right. At least it's a plan. Here, swap guns." Jesse took the one that belonged to the still-unconscious man on the barn floor. He wiped it clean with a blue shop towel he'd stuck under the front seat. "This is a .45. Why would he have a .45? No police force carries .45s anymore." He turned the pistol over, studying it one last time, and then stuffed the gun down the front of the man's underwear where it would be out of reach. The man would have to be related to Houdini to get to it. Jesse put the remainder of their stuff back into the car and closed the trunk.

"Are you ready? If he is a terrorist, we may be driving into an ambush. Maybe you should be lying on the floor in back," Jesse said, worried stiff. "It might be safer there unless they shoot me and I crash the car."

"Look, you said I was your gal. We're in this together, right?" Then, being more practical, Leena said, "Two sets of eyes are better than one, and I swear if someone shoots at us I'm going to blast their freaking head off."

He knew she was afraid, but she had already demonstrated that she was no coward. He just hoped it wouldn't be a cop if anyone started shooting at them. He aimed the car straight down the lane. "You ready for this?"

She nodded, eyes open and focused.

The car shot down the lane as fast as he could reasonably go and keep control. When he came to the road, he spun the steering wheel hard left and the car responded beautifully. A trail of dust came spewing onto the road.

There was no need. They were alone on the road, no other cars in sight.

After a few minutes of silence, they both started to speak at the same time. He shut up as Leena said, "I have an idea. Let's stop at a busy gas station and instead of calling the sheriff, we'll call the FBI. Maybe you should talk to them. Just tell them there's a foreigner with a phony sheriff's badge tied up in a barn. Tell them where the barn is. Afterward, just hang up. The FBI records every call so you only have to tell them once."

"After that, what? We just get on the road and go?"

"Yeah, why not? You already said it: we'd have to stick around. We'll never get to California on time for our meet with WCN if we wait around for the police to do their thing." Leena spotted a cop car approaching from up ahead. "And watch your speed. When we get on the Interstate, I'll call my boss. Maybe he can give us some advice. And, uh, by the way, nice neighborhood you grew up in. Peaceful. Quiet."

Perturbed, he looked straight ahead. What could he say?

They stopped at a gas station and after using the facilities, checked to make sure no surveillance cameras pointed their way. While he called the local area FBI and gave somebody the cover story they'd dreamed up, Leena ducked into a Starbucks and bought breakfast sweets and coffee. As they were getting back onto the toll road, they saw another cop car sitting by the ramp. The two cops inside were staring down cars passing by. When they went by, one of the cops waved at them.

He wasn't sure if that were good or bad. Maybe they'd seen him and Leena on the news. "I wonder what's going on. There seem to be a lot of cops out today," he said as they stopped to pick up a toll ticket.

"I'm going to call the network," she said as he increased speed and headed onto the highway.

Jesse heard the surprise in her voice several times before she finally hung up. She hadn't said anything about their dilemma.

"Homeland Security declared a Threat Level Red this morning."

"Did those animals crash another jet into a building?" he blurted out.

"No, nothing like that. It's the usual: lots of terrorist chatter, nothing specific."

"So that's why there are so many cops out."

"Probably." Leena sipped her coffee and looked out the window at the passing farmland, oddly uncommunicative.

"So what did your boss have to say?" he asked, after he'd had a minute to eat a sweet roll.

"He wasn't in and Kellie, my office assistant, said he'd gone to a special meeting with reps from four of the largest oil companies. They suddenly want to advertise with us."

"And that means?" he asked, but already knew the answer.

"They probably want to kill the story in exchange for millions in advertising."

"Has your network ever done that before?"

"Not to my knowledge, but it's common practice at many of the others. Their motto should be 'Pay us or we'll go after you'. Ever notice they never go after any of the companies that advertise on their stations?"

"Isn't that blackmail or coercion?"

"Sure it is, but who are the advertisers going to report it to? You've seen what the left-leaning networks can do to the most powerful man in the world, the president. Little bits make big gobs. One snippet at a time and they have his popularity rating down in the thirty-percent range. People who used to love him…the networks have them hating him now."

"Yeah, I see, but what does that have to do with us? Wait a minute. The red alert, big oil, and that…that *man* back in the barn." He could not bring himself to say cop. "Could that all have to do with us?" Not waiting for her answer, he plunged ahead. "What was it that guy said about shooting, but not killing me?"

"He said they wanted to take you alive. I wonder who 'they' are. Hey, and what's with you kicking the shit out of that guy? Got an anger issue?"

"No. Well…maybe. I just can't stand people pointing guns at me. Probably goes back to when I fought in the war. I mean, just thinking about it pisses me off."

"Calm down, big guy. I've been thinking of something else. How did they find us so easily?"

"I've been wondering about that, too. I was tired when I pulled into the lane last night. But still, I think I would have noticed a car following us. It was late, and the roads were deserted."

"There are only two or three possibilities. One, somehow they tailed us. I agree that seems unlikely. Two, someone recognized you on TV and guessed you'd be going home. That seems even more remote. Three, they planted a homing device somewhere on the car. That seems most likely, and they could be listening to us right now." Leena raised her voice and put up her hands. "Hello, creeps!" Seeing Jesse's face, she said, "What? It's a little too late to be keeping quiet now."

"How about a fourth possibility," Jesse suggested, and it was Leena's turn to look perplexed. He pointed up. "Couldn't they track us by satellite?"

"Our own country?"

"You just finished telling me how the TV networks could corrupt the best of companies. Why couldn't some of the big businesses buy off the U.S. government?"

"You're getting too paranoid. We have to trust in something. If it were true about satellites tracking us, wouldn't it be more likely they'd be Russian? Their economy is very much vested in oil."

"Russian. Yeah, I suppose anything's possible. But listen," he said in the most serious voice he could muster, "this is supposed to be a fun trip for you. It seems to have changed into a very dangerous one. Chicago is only about fifty miles ahead. I can drop you off at O'Hare Airport and you can catch a flight back to New York this afternoon."

"You do have an issue with trust, don't you? But who would save your butt next time?" She crossed her arms. "You owe me. I'm going to San Francisco with or without you. And as a matter of fact, it's about time that I get to drive this beast."

He looked at her and smiled for the first time that day. "Okay, can you wait until we get through Chicago? Maybe in the meantime, we should both start thinking of a plan. But, uh, quietly, just in case someone is listening."

She responded by holding his hand. She had to move the pistol that was on the seat next to his leg. "You might still be trainable."

He noticed she reset the safety on the pistol, for now.

They continued on Interstate 80 and drove straight through Chicago. The traffic was horrid. There were tons of cops out. It was early afternoon when they decided to stop for lunch at a small town just west of Joliet. They ordered fast food and then stopped at a Wal-Mart for some supplies for the car. While Leena shopped, Jesse made a thorough inspection of the car for a transmitter bug. He'd never seen a bug and really didn't know what he was searching for, but he did know what was supposed to be on the car. There wasn't anything weird on the exterior of the Take-Us. They'd always kept the doors locked to keep the curious out, and there was no sign of forced entry. He checked the interior briefly, thinking there was no way a bug could be inside the car. He grimaced, not knowing if that made him happy or not.

Chapter 11

The Senator's Quest

The pictures on his office wall reminded Senator Benjamin Charlton of the tremendous amount of power his family had exerted over the past fifty years. Even though many of his brothers were dead, all had served their country with honor and distinction. That gave him a sense of guilt every time he thought about it. He rationalized that they had served in a different time. If they were alive now, they'd have to do the same things he did.

Charlton reached into one of the drawers of his solid walnut desk and brought out a green bottle of scotch. He leaned back into his rich leather chair and took a swig straight out of the bottle. That ought to start my motor, he thought, and then poured some more into the #1 DAD coffee cup his youngest daughter had given him for his birthday last year. She was the only good thing that had come out of his last marriage. He checked his watch: two more hours to kill before he had to be at the foreign intelligence committee meeting.

The senator looked down at his phone when it rang, immediately noticing the light blinking, indicating that it was a call on his private line. There were only a handful of people who had the private number. He hoped.

"Yes," he said, bringing the phone close to his ear.

"Ben, this is Jane, how are you?"

"Jane, where have you been?" he asked of the voice he'd never heard before.

"I've been traveling, on business mostly, and have just arrived back in town."

He hesitated just for a moment. Jane. Back in town. What was the correct response? Then, through the fog, he remembered. "Jane, I haven't seen you in months."

"Okay, then. How about we meet for drinks tonight at the usual time, same place as last time?" she suggested, being as vague as she could possibly be.

"I can't wait to see you again," he said truthfully, because the Chinese always knew what to bring to the meeting afterward.

He was just starting to ponder what the Chinese wanted from him this time when the phone rang again, the same private line. What could she have forgotten?

"Yes?" he asked once again.

"Benny, this is Bradford Givings up here in New York. How have you been?"

"Brad, this is a real surprise. I'm doing fine. Thanks for asking." He sat up straighter in his leather chair. "What can I do for you?"

"Listen, I'm on my way to the airport as we speak, and I'd like to get together as soon as possible. How about this afternoon, say two o'clock?"

"I have an important meeting this afternoon, foreign intelligence. Could we do it later?"

"Actually, no. This is more important. I'm sure you can get out of your committee meeting if you have to, correct?"

"Of course. I'll arrange it."

"I'll send a limo."

"No problem. See you then." After carefully putting the phone down, he again reached into his desk for the bottle and this time took two deep swallows. What could the Arabs want? First the Chinese and now Brad. He pushed the intercom button on his phone and immediately his executive secretary's voice came over the phone.

"Yes, sir?"

"What's going on, Joyce?"

"I don't understand, sir."

"What's going on in the world, like the Middle East or China, for instance?"

"I don't know about the Middle East, per se, but this morning the Department of Homeland Security put us on Threat Level Red."

"Red? What the hell does that mean? I thought that was just a gimmick we created for the little people."

Joyce sighed. "Let me transfer you to Eileen." Her voice held a hint of disgust as she added, "She has a source at DHS. I think she's been in contact with her source today."

"Forget that. Tell her to come to my office."

A few minutes later a dumpy, little woman closed the door behind her, walked over, and took a seat in front of Charlton's desk.

"Good morning, Senator," Eileen said in a Northeast accent, her nose wrinkling at the smell of whiskey permeating the room.

It seemed like it was hard to find good-looking help anymore, the senator mused. Probably because of that last sex allegation. He thought he'd quietly taken care of it. But still, the word gets around. "Good morning, Ellen, what do you have?"

"Eileen, sir—"

"Sorry, of course, Eileen. So much on my mind."

"It's okay. Well, Senator, after I saw the news this morning, I called a friend of mine over at Homeland Security."

"Yes, yes," the senator said, impatient to get to the point, his head buzzing from the snort of whiskey he'd taken right before she arrived in his office.

"My friend said they positively don't have any idea what's going on. The activity has increased to a level they've never experienced before. The one concrete thing she did tell me was that they have a number of suspected terrorist cells that just went 'hot' in the last few hours."

"How many, exactly?"

"She didn't know exactly. When I pressed her if it was more than half a dozen, she said yes."

He leaned forward, smiling, thinking he could give that to Brad. "Issh there anything happening in Sshina?"

"China?" She smelled the booze on his breath and realized he was already drunk and couldn't even hold one thought. "I haven't heard a thing this morning. I could check, but I don't recall hearing anything." She shook her head sadly, wondering what happened to the man who used to be the Last Great White Liberal Hope.

"Thanks, Ellen. If you hear any more, let me know, okay? Right away."

After she departed, Charlton figured he'd have to sniff around a little. It was harder to get secret information than it used to be, ever since the FBI found out that the Chinese had acquired the technology for their missile systems from one of the committees he sat on. He was, of course, far too powerful to be implicated. But it was odd. Recently, it seemed that the leadership on both sides of the aisle didn't trust him with secrets.

* * *

The chauffeur closed the door behind the senator.

"Benny, it's good to see you again," Bradford F. Givings said, reaching for a green bottle from the small bar installed in the back of the limousine. "How about a drink?"

The senator had already decided he wouldn't have anything more to drink, but one couldn't hurt, could it? He found himself saying, "One couldn't hurt, could it?" in what sounded to him like an echo.

"So, Senator, do you ever watch the news?"

"Are you referring to the red alert?"

"No, not that. However, what about it?"

"Homeland Security has their eyes on about six, or was it sixteen, secret, or maybe hidden, cells that just came to life."

"Interesting! No, what I wanted to know is if you saw the report WCN carried last night."

"WCN? No way. They hate me. It's a conservative network and I'm hardly conservative. I only watch CNN or one of the others. It doesn't matter which one. they're all our friends and they all report the same thing."

"So you never heard of the Take-Us car?"

"The what?" The senator took a long slurp of his drink.

"The owner calls it the Take-Us automobile. We don't know

why he named it that, yet."

"Is it some kind of weapon or something?"

That brought forth a laugh from the New York lawyer. "In a way I suppose it is, but not in the traditional sense. It's an electrically powered car that's supposed to make its own power as it drives down the road. I brought a DVD of the interview for you to watch. And what I need you to do is use the enormous power of the United States government to find out everything you can about it and the guy who invented it. We don't even know how to spell his last name."

"How am I shupposhed to do that?"

"We thought of that for you. If it were true that this car could travel without using any gasoline, then the government would lose the revenue from the gas tax that's collected at the pump. I'm sure you remember"—he looked hard at the old drunk—"that the revenues are supposed to go toward road maintenance and new road construction. Therefore you, being the federal government, would have to find another way of replacing the income you'd lose. That would mean new taxes, and you know how you and your party love to raise taxes."

"So this car really works? We could tax it?"

"We assume so. However, in fact, this is your excuse to find the man for me."

"Whatever you shay…issh your money." The senator forgot to ask the most important question: why was Mr. Bradford F. Givings of New York City so interested in finding this Take-Us car?

* * *

Senator Charlton was almost delirious with possibilities when he returned to the Capitol. By being the first one in his party to think of a new way to raise taxes, after all this time, he was suddenly going to be relevant again.

His office staff also became somewhat unglued with excitement after Senator Charlton outlined his new plan to them. There was a sense of direction and action that had been missing for quite some time. The nonstop ringing of the phones was so invigorating he almost forgot his other appointment that night. It was only after finishing the bottle of scotch in his desk—and still needing another drink—that he remembered.

Charlton stood at a bar located near the Watergate Hotel, gratefully sipping his first drink when a very pretty Asian girl with long, black hair sashayed up.

"Ben, darling, how good to see you again," she said, standing on her tiptoes to give him a hug.

With what little that was left of his alcoholic brain, the senator recognized that the Chinese were brilliant in the way they ran their espionage program. He never met the same agent twice, and they were all named Jane.

"Like I said on the phone, I just got back in town. I'm glad we could get together tonight."

"I'm a-glad to see you, too," he slurred.

"Come on," she said, grabbing his hand and leading him away with a gentle sway of her hips. "I have a booth over there." She nodded in the general direction of the back wall where through the gloom of the darkly lit room it appeared that most of the booths were already occupied.

After they sat down, she put one arm around his neck and gave him a kiss. With her other hand reached under the table and grabbed his crotch. They finished the kiss.

"I take it we have a room here," he whispered in her ear.

"Of course."

"Let's go, then."

"Not yet, silly boy. First buy me a couple of drinks so I can appear to get drunk," she whispered back, sticking her tongue deep in his ear.

They sat at the table drinking for a while. Then she reached into her purse, opened a brown prescription bottle, and shook out a handful of small, blue pills. "Take these. I'm told they take some time before they start working. We can talk awhile."

They talked nonsense for an hour before walking out.

The senator stepped unsteadily through the doorway into the

hotel suite. All these rooms appeared the same, he thought…soulless.

She crossed in front of him, sat down at the couch, and gestured for him to sit beside her. He picked up the drink already on the small table and sipped. He could feel the heat rising from below his beltline and looked forward to the next phase of the meeting with increased anticipation.

"Ssso, what can I help you with? You do know that re-election is coming up next year. I'll need a tall stack of cash for that."

"Have we ever let you down? You have delivered and we have kept our end of the agreement. Now we need something else from you."

"Ever since I got the rocket telemetry information, most of my top-secret sources have dried up or gone to prison. Someone must have spread the word that I was no longer trustworthy," the liberal senator whined into his drink.

"We've noticed the same thing, but this is something entirely different. You have perhaps heard about this new type of automobile…I believe it is called the Take-Us, an electrically propelled automobile."

"Heard of it? I watched a DVD of the interview in my office."

"Where did you get a copy?"

He reached down and tapped the ice cubes in his drink, temporarily submerging them. "A friend dropped it by."

"A friend named Givings of New York?"

The senator raised his eyebrows. "He thought that I might be interested in the legislative aspect of the car."

"Who is bullshitting who? Givings works for the Arabs."

"What can I say? It's very expensive running for re-election." He took another swallow from his drink. "I have to do whatever I can to raise money," he said without a trace of guilt.

"It can also be very dangerous working both sides of the street, or should I say three sides? And now with the Russians, it is four sides," she said abruptly. "What do the Arabs want?"

"The same thing you want, information on this car thingy."

"What did you give them so far?"

He was too drunk to weigh the implications of his next statement. "I told 'em that Homelan' Security has got…has seen…at least a half dozen…or maybe it was a dozen…whatever. A bunch of sleeper cells have gone crazy. They haven't put it all togezzer yet. Hey, wait, izzat what the red alert is about?"

She ignored the question. "Where are these cells located?"

"I don't have that infor…informmayshun yet. I'm not sure I'll ever know."

"What else?"

"Nothin', jus' that I, uh…I've assigned all of my shtaff to call in ever' favor that's owed and to find out ever'sing they can about this Chris…Chris…da guy and his car."

"So you don't really know anything. Here let me get you another." She got up and walked across the room to the bar, gave a signal, and two girls who were in the bedroom came out. Both were attractive Chinese girls dressed in identical black negligees. They could have been twins.

"I also have a special treat for you," Jane said from across the room and gestured toward the bedroom. A young boy came out of the room, dressed only in a short, black silk robe.

By now, both girls were on the couch laughing and chatting away, massaging and rubbing the senator.

Charlton looked at the boy and said, "Are you sure iss safe? I godda be ext' careful these days."

"Of course. He doesn't even speak English," Jane said, laughing and looking over to the bedroom door. She moved her hand from the first bottle to the marked bottle behind the bar. "I also have some special magic dust for you." She showed him a sugar bowl full of cocaine.

He hardly heard her, his hand under one of the girl's negligees, the other girl busy with the belt to his pants. The boy took the drink, the cocaine, and a mirror over to him. Charlton drank noisily as the boy made lines on the mirror, which the senator sucked up inelegantly, barely able to see.

Senator Charlton was not a young man, having just celebrated his sixty-sixth birthday. The Viagra started to work after the senator did his first line of coke, and he believed himself to have been reborn as a proud stallion.

The boy put the mirror under his nose a second time and Charlton did another fat line. The girls had undressed him. The young boy knelt down and took Charlton's penis into his mouth. The tempo of the sexual activity increased, faster and faster. The senator began breathing heavily, then gasped for breath. He tried to sit up, choking out the words, "Air, I can't breathe."

The girl on the left put her breast into his mouth, making it harder to get any air. Charlton seemed paralyzed, couldn't even struggle.

The booze, the cocaine, and the drugs—including the one he couldn't taste that Jane had put into his last drink—all came together. His heart, working hard to keep up, just came apart, like an egg dropped onto a marble floor.

Jane, whose name was actually Janae, walked over and peered at the lifeless body and said in Chinese, "Take this condom and do what I told you earlier."

Janae walked back into the bedroom and said to her superior, Jaeho Lee, "Are you sure this is necessary?"

Jaeho Lee was neither tall nor short, thin nor fat. His face seemed to put his age between twenty and forty, nondescript and average, a perfect cover for an intelligence operative. They watched as both girls rolled the senator over and the boy took a condom out and smeared some KY jelly on it.

"They know what to do," Jaeho said, turning to face Janae. "You must always remember. First, a man betrays himself. Next his country. After that he will sell himself to the highest bidder. His god has become money."

"I understand that. But why leave him in such disgrace?"

"Did you see how easily he gave up the Arabs? He has lost control and can no longer keep his mouth closed. He would sell us out next. Besides, he has lost the trust of his fellow senators. Better this way. We already have a new junior senator in place. In a few years he will have access to even better information. In America, you can buy anything."

"But why did he have to go this way?" Janae asked and then, seeing they had finished, said from the doorway, "All right, clean this place up, leave the lines of coke on the mirror, don't forget to take the tainted bottle, and place his first glass on the table."

"Yes, okay. We know what to do," the young male agent said, and then proudly switched to English. "Take a chilled pill or something."

"It's chill pill," Janae said. Looking over her shoulder at Jaeho, she added, "He is very impertinent."

"He is young and still learning. They will be on a flight back to China in a few hours and out of reach." Jaeho reached over and tenderly touched Janae's shoulder. "You cannot assassinate a senator of his stature without some kind of investigation. This way, the family will stop the inquest and insist on keeping it quiet after the initial investigation shows some of the sordid details to them."

"Yes, the family does not want to be disgraced." She lowered her eyes. "What about this Take-Us car? It was obvious that he knew nothing."

"Is it not also obvious that we must find it? And soon. I fear others have an insurmountable lead."

Chapter 12

The Dirt Within

Agent Mike Nowiki of the Federal Bureau of Investigation was standing at the foot of the hospital bed when he heard the door open behind him. He turned and saw the large, uniformed figure of Sheriff Charles Trojanowski strutting through the doorway.

"Hey, Chuck, good to see you again," the FBI Agent said, offering his hand.

"Mike. How you been?" the sheriff asked, looking down on the shorter and always nervous agent. "How's Linda's knee doin'?" Their wives played on the same women's slow-pitch softball team.

"It's getting better. I wish a little faster. I'm getting tired of all the extra honey-do lists."

"Yeah, I know what you mean. So what's the big secret? All I was told is that you wanted me to come to the hospital by myself."

"Is he one of yours?" Mike stepped aside so the sheriff had a better view of the man lying on the bed.

It took the sheriff a moment to recognize the man. He had a large, angry bruise running along one side of his face. A bandage wrapped vertically around his head held his jaw shut. His right arm was in a splint.

"That's Deputy Ali Assad," the sheriff said, dropping his hand onto the butt of his gun, his anger rising. "Why wasn't I notified sooner?"

"Easy, Chuck. We received an anonymous call this morning telling us he was at an abandoned barn outside of Mishawaka, on the north side. The caller said Assad here might be a terrorist." The FBI agent looked directly into the taller man's eyes. "As you know, the country went on an elevated threat level this morning, so we jumped on this right away. Any idea what he would be doing over there?"

"North side of Mishawaka? That's where I live…No, I don't know. He's assigned to jail duty, and he's only been with the department for maybe two or three years."

"Was he working undercover on anything?"

"No way. We don't let new deputies do that for a few more years. Why?"

"When we found him he was bound hand and foot with white plastic wire ties. He also had a Colt .45 in his underwear, probably shoved down there by whoever beat the shit out of him. But the gun had the serial numbers filed off. It had also been fired. One round was missing, and we found a spent casing on the floor."

"Any blood?"

"Just his. Very little, just from his mouth."

"What are you not telling me?"

The FBI agent took a deep breath. "When we searched the surrounding area, we found a Honda Accord with Michigan plates about a quarter mile away. The keys were in his pocket. We searched the car and found his service weapon and uniform in the trunk. We also found a briefcase. We forced the lock, and inside we found a laptop computer, three cell phones, and two passports: one from Canada and the other from Mexico. They both had Assad's picture, but each had a different name on it."

"When he wakes up, maybe we should ask him," the sheriff said in a gruff tone.

"The doctor wants to keep him unconscious for a couple more days due to the seriousness of his head injuries. Then we have a different problem."

"What's that?"

"His jaw is broken and will be wired shut. He won't be able to speak for at least a month, more like six weeks."

"Maybe he can type left-handed." The sheriff walked over and collapsed into a chair beside the bed. "A few years back, a grand jury had a complaint and then HQ did a study. The results were that the department wasn't diversified enough. When we hired Assad, I remember thinking: here's this young guy from Iran, single, a Muslim, with no real background we could check. I believe he was a political refugee or something. He could have fit the profile—oops, we don't use that word anymore—of any of the 9/11 terrorists."

"How did he get around the screening process?"

"You tell me. We use the FBI to do background checks."

"Yeah, but, that's just one of the steps, right?"

"He was an immigrant and we had to have a body to show our good faith in fulfilling our quota. He probably slipped through the cracks somehow." The sheriff put his head in his hands. "This is not good."

"I think I know what you're thinking. I have a suggestion. When we checked him in, we just gave his name as John Doe. With your consent, we'll put him in federal protective custody. I can have a couple of federal marshals here in a few hours. When the doctors clear him, we'll move him to a federal facility. All you have to do is give him to us on temporary duty. Or if that's too difficult, give him a vacation."

"If he's a terrorist, what then?"

"We try to turn him. If he won't change sides, he'll probably be sent to Club Gitmo."

"And if he's not a terrorist?"

"Come on, Chuck. What do you smell here?"

"Yeah, I suppose," the sheriff said with a look of resignation. He got up to leave. "One last thing. Who did this to him? Any clue?"

"Not yet. We didn't find much at the barn. We do have the voiceprint of the 9-1-1 call, and when we notify Washington and they inform Homeland Security, we can expect a small army of agents to investigate. I'm sure they'll give it their highest priority, especially with this elevated alert we're on now."

"You don't think this is in any way connected to that, do you?"

"I don't know, but I'm pretty sure he wasn't there to blow up the barn. I'm afraid this is only the beginning of a very long road that we are both going to travel."

Chapter 13

The Evil Threat

Lieutenant Mustafa Kourani stood at loose attention in front of the desk, his eyes fixed straight ahead. He had never seen the heavy curtains open. It was always dark in this office that smelled of stale tobacco smoke and coffee. The officer seated behind the desk was the most brutal man he had ever come to know, but for whatever reason, Colonel Mafsanjani seemed to be placing Kourani under his direct supervision, teaching him all the subtle things that he'd need to excel in this command. Kourani said a silent prayer to Allah, hoping the colonel wouldn't require any sexual acts from him.

"Very well, Lieutenant, I must inquire. Is there any news from your brother Mahmoud? You may stand at ease."

"Mahmoud?" He relaxed a little...very little. "Sir, he is in prison in America."

"Yes, yes, I know that. I have his file right here." Mafsanjani picked it up and began reading from it. "This is a newspaper article from *The Detroit News*. It says, 'Mahmoud was trained in weaponry, spy-craft, and counterintelligence in Lebanon and Iran'"—and then skimming ahead—"and 'was a member, fighter, recruiter, and fund-raiser for Hezbollah'..."

Colonel Mafsanjani exhaled. He seemed to be short of breath lately, probably too many cigarettes. "That was written in May 2003. The newspaper got part of it right. He's one of us. We sent him to America to set up a group of cells, which by the way, he was extremely successful at."

"My father receives a letter every few months, saying that he is doing well and is extremely busy," Kourani offered. "My father thinks he means that American prisons are good places to recruit new fighters to our cause."

"Yes, that is so." Mafsanjani closed the file, picked up a stale, cold cup of coffee, and took a sip. He already knew about the letters to his father. He had a copy of each in his file. "Do you know Ali Assad? You are about the same age."

"Yes, of course, sir. We are from the same village. He is a cousin of mine."

"You know, then, that he is also in America?"

"No, sir. I did not know that. I only knew that his family moved out of the village many years ago."

"I tell you this in the greatest secrecy, Mustafa. Ali was under your brother's command, at least until prison interrupted, and worked at a very important post. Last night in America, he was sent on a mission and has not been heard from since. I tell you this because if he was arrested, the Americans will try to make him talk. As is normal in cases like this, he will try to get word back to his family in your village, telling them to flee. That is, after all, how we guarantee his loyalty. If that were to transpire, you will get word to me immediately. I will guarantee your family's safety. Is that clear?"

"Yes, sir." The young lieutenant stood to attention again, stiff as an all-night hard on.

"Good. You understand." A couple seconds later, the colonel said, "You want to ask something?"

"Sir. Exactly what mission was Ali on?"

"Spoken like a good intelligence officer. That is good. It is a mission that"—the colonel suddenly coughed and then curled his thin lips into what he probably thought was a smile. He pointed a finger at the portrait of the Iranian president—"the rabid little dog wants accomplished."

Mafsanjani stopped speaking, picked up another cigarette, and tapped it on the desk. "If all goes well, I will tell you sometime. Go get some sleep. It is nearly three o'clock in the morning. You are dismissed."

Kourani departed, his mind racing. I am going to be killed for something my cousin did half a world away, he thought. Wait until my American friend on the student committee hears about this. Maybe I can get a warning to my father. So help me Allah, we have to change this government!

Mafsanjani went to work on his computer after Kourani left. Along with everything else, the Internet had changed the intelligence business forever. He could give orders to his agents everywhere from his office in Tehran. Email and instant messenger were his favorite choices. They were routed to servers in Europe and South America. No longer would an agent have to figure out a way to smuggle information out of a country. They just downloaded, uploaded, and reloaded or whatever term you wanted to use.

One of the advantages of this system was that agents in the same cell could live across the street from one another and never know they worked for the same employer. Each cell was composed of three men. No women belonged to a cell. The only time the members were exposed was when the cell went active. If somehow the agents were taken alive or arrested, each man would know only the names given to him by the other two. The only downfall was for security. After each mission the cells had to be dissolved and reorganized. The different American intelligence agencies watched individual members, but had no hard evidence unless they caught them going active.

Mafsanjani looked hard at the list in front of him. He compared it to the likely route the car would take. He decided which cells to activate and then, with a series of keystrokes, awoke eighteen sleepers. Six complete cells. Now that they were active they would be known as units. He had made a critical mistake with Ali. He should have ordered him to wait for the entire cell to arrive, but the other two members, although en route, had been too far away to help.

Mafsanjani also had the lawyer, even though Givens wasn't officially on his payroll. OPEC had a way of making things right.

This was much too important a mission to trust to his underlings. He would be the controlling officer on this mission. His orders were the same as before. Capture the man if possible, and if not, kill him. The woman he didn't care about. They could have a little fun and then behead her. That always seemed to piss off the Great Satan more than anything else.

Chapter 14

DHS—The Fleeting Impression

"Deputy Director Gustoffson," Patrick O'Hallohan nearly shouted as he came into Gustoffson's office. "We got a live one!"

"O'Hallohan, how long have we known each other? I told you to call me Gus."

"Sorry, sir, I mean, Gus. Sir, it's the military training, I suppose."

"Forget it. We have a live what?"

"Terrorist."

"Do tell."

"The FBI in Indiana found him. A Mr. Ali Assad—correct that: *Deputy Sheriff* Ali Assad."

"A sheriff?"

"The report I received is really sketchy. Apparently, they found him in a deserted barn. He was pretty badly beaten up. He's still out, or rather unconscious."

"Who did the beating?"

"No one seems to know."

"When we find out, let's give him a friggin' medal. Let me see that." Gustoffson stuck out his hand. After he finished reading the report, he looked up at Patrick. "Where in Indiana is this town?"

"The northern part of the state, almost in Michigan. South Bend is right next to it."

"South Bend. Isn't that where Notre Dame University is located? What are they going to do, blow up the Golden Dome and start a real religious war? Anything else around there worth blowing up?"

"Just the usual malls, schools, and some small defense contractors, but Chicago is only eighty miles away. Might be a staging ground."

"For what? The Sears Tower? I thought we put that to rest a few years ago," Gustoffson said with a wave of his hand.

"We might have, but did they?" Patrick pointed to a picture of one of the Twin Towers coming down on the wall behind the director's desk.

"Good point. Get that region briefed. Non-specific, just tell them to be extra vigilant. You can give this to the press, but not a word about our deputy. I thought you were pulled from the night duty officers' shift?"

"Can't help it, sir. I'm caught up in it. I can almost smell the stink coming from this one."

"You're the only Rapid Response Team leader we have. Don't get too worn out. Your team might need to get involved in this sooner or later."

After O'Hallohan left, Gustoffson turned back to his computer and pulled up a map showing all potential targets that Homeland Security had preliminarily identified in the South Bend region. There didn't appear to be anything out of the ordinary about the area. No military bases or large defense contractors. A few bridges, no big dams. The only thing prominently noticeable was the toll road. I-80 and I-90 traversed through there. Even in Iraq, they didn't blow up highways just for the hell of it.

He went through the different reports on top of his desk, from domestic to military and even foreign surveillance agencies like the British and Israelis. He viewed the different stories from news-gathering organizations: AP, Reuters, Fox, and so forth. There wasn't anything exceptional going on out there that was much different from the previous week. The only thing he could figure is that terrorists seemed to have a thing about dates and numbers. And tomorrow was 6/11.

Chapter 15

The Strange Friend

Jesse felt like he was in a trance, foggy from lack of sleep. He'd been driving since early in the morning. It was now just before four in the afternoon, New York time. That was three o'clock Central time where they were in Iowa. He turned the Take-Us off the Interstate and pulled into the rest area.

"I gotta go," Leena said, smiling. "You were right when you said this car can only go as far as your bladder can hold."

"I did say that. However, there are other limitations. Like, I am sooooo stiff and sore, I need to walk around a bit. I'm not used to sitting so much."

"What about when you were driving to New York?" she asked, as he pulled in and parked.

He opened the door and creaked his way slowly out of the car. "Nobody was out to shoot me back then. That seems like ten years ago, not just—was that this morning?"

"Time-warp morning." She narrowed her eyes and looked slightly harder.

"Yeah, I suppose." Jesse glanced around the parking lot.

***

The sun was hot on his face when Leena strode out of the women's restroom. Her smile was gone and her eyes had a hardened look to them. Once again she had her cell phone plastered to her ear. "No, I don't want you to call the sheriff's office and check."

They turned and started to walk steadily in the thick, spring grass toward the end of the rest area. "Are you absolutely sure?" she asked into the phone. A Greyhound bus went noisily by and Jesse couldn't hear her next few words before she clicked her phone shut.

"My assistant says the red alert warning is concentrated on the Chicago, Detroit, and immediate area. I think it is about us."

"Now who's getting paranoid?"

She dropped his hand and spun around to look at him, face to face. He didn't even realize they were holding hands, it felt so natural.

"My assistant called our local affiliate station, and they have no information on any police officers being injured today." And then, like an assault rifle on full automatic, she blurted out, "Where was his police car? Why did he sneak up on us and want to shoot you? How come he didn't have a radio with him and…why did he have to look just like someone from the fucking Middle East?"

"You may be right," he said, looking down into pure fire, tears alight in her eyes. "When I called the FBI, I did give them some reason to doubt. They'll probably have to conduct an investigation," he said, more calmly than he felt. "If he's innocent, they'd try to protect his reputation. If he's guilty, they'd keep it as quiet as possible to cover their own asses. Either way, what can we do about it? Are you okay?"

"Really, I'm not having a meltdown. It's just the reporter in me wants to go back and dig for the answers. Well…maybe a little melt."

"I think we should just keep driving." He stroked her cheek.

She reached up and put her arms around him and he completed the circle by wrapping his arms around her. They stood like that for several minutes.

"Okay," she whispered softly, the fire back under control. "You're very good at this part, you know." She gave him a deep, soft kiss.

"You're pretty good at that part, too" he said when the kiss ended.

"Pretty good! I'm sure you meant the best." She looked up at him, a slow smile spreading across her face. "It's my turn to drive."

"What? Give you the keys?" He broke the embrace and started to run away.

"Come back, you chicken, or I'll beat you up," she yelled, running after him.

He stopped abruptly and let her run straight into his arms. They fell to the ground on a bed of soft grass, and he didn't care who was watching them.

* * *

Jesse opened his eyes and watched Leena without her being aware. He was so exhausted he'd slept all the way to Omaha. Leena had been driving for more than three hundred miles, and she looked like she just awoke from a good night's sleep. She was such a beautiful woman. The new forties…she looked to be in her late twenties.

He was feeling pretty dang good, maybe even a little feisty. It crossed his mind that when something so dramatic, almost catastrophic, happens to you—and once you have a chance to put some sleep and miles behind you—it makes you feel almost invincible all over again.

Jesse sat up, slid over, and kissed Leena on the cheek. He could smell her perfume. "Thanks for driving. I was bushed."

"It's been great," she said, the bright sunlight reflecting off her sunglasses from the setting sun. "I can't remember the last time I drove this car. Now, it's so quiet. People living next to busy roads are really going to appreciate this car."

"Does it drive any differently from the last time?"

"I know you might not want to hear this but, well…no."

He burst into laughter. "It's weird, but that's the best thing you could have said. The key to having a smooth transition from an old technology to a new and better one is that it doesn't feel any different. No shock effect, at least not at first. Incrementalism, that's the ticket."

"Sometimes I can't tell if you're serious or just goofy."

"What?"

"Incrementalism? Are you sure that's even a word?"

He took a drink of warm water from the bottle. "I'm as sure of it as I am of the word *flotistacia*."

"Flott—? What?"

"Flott-i-stay-shuh. It means the last flat, stale, mouthful of liquid, usually beer, in the bottom of the bottle."

"Really, I never heard of that before."

Jesse burst out laughing. "Yeah, well, I invented that word."

"I knew that wasn't a word." She reached over and punched him in the arm. She was laughing just as hard as he was. "You sure are full of it when you get some good sleep."

"I am full of it," he admitted. "It feels good just to be alive."

"All this driving makes my head tired, but my body feels full of energy," Leena said.

Jesse subconsciously glanced down at the cleavage that was showing above the sleeveless top she was wearing.

Catching his glance, Leena said in a deep, sexy voice, "Maybe we'll have to figure out a way of burning all this excess energy off."

He took her hand. "Maybe this time we should go to the motel first, before we get something to eat."

"Well, it's never good to eat a heavy meal before vigorous exercise," she said. "Something light, like a salad, would be good."

He caught the hint of promise in her voice.

* * *

They stopped for dinner at what Leena called a brand-name restaurant, where the food is never good or bad. In spite of what she said, he decided he needed something a little more substantial than a salad.

"You know I'm twice your size, so that means I need twice the food," he explained to her.

"Twice would be nice," she said, way too innocently.

Service was slow and while they were waiting they saw an older couple shuffling toward their table. The man held the woman's arm protectively and held her chair out for her. He then gave her a kiss on the cheek after she was seated.

"Isn't that just darling," Leena said.

"Love without sex, the greatest," he said.

"Why do you say that?"

"The way I see it, there are three stages, nowadays, in relationships." Leena tilted her head as Jesse continued. "Stage one is when you have sex without love. Stage two, when you have love and sex together. Stage three is when you get older. The sex parts don't work so well any longer, and you have love without sex. To me this seems like the ultimate and perfect end to a genuine loving relationship."

"Why did you say 'nowadays'?"

"In yesteryear couples were engaged for years and years before they got married. Maybe back then they were already deeply in love before they started out their marriages. Love without sex."

"You don't believe in love at first sight?"

"More like lust at first sight." He looked again at her cleavage.

"Then what is your time frame?" She pulled up the front of her top. "How long does it take to fall in love?"

"I don't know..." He sensed he was getting in trouble. "I think that would depend on many factors. But what I'm saying is that in the modern world people want to test drive everything before they commit, and lust is the primary motivating factor in beginning relationships."

"I like sex and we're not young kids." She looked him straight in the eye. "We have spent the last eight months talking to each other about everything under the sun except this subject. I don't know if I love you or not, but it seems that all the right pieces are there. If you want to 'test drive' me, then I'm all for it. I see it as the next step forward in a long-term relationship." She gave him a passionate kiss and stuck her tongue deep in his mouth.

When he came up for air all he could say was, "You're right. Maybe we are in stage two." He was ready to jump under the table with her right then. He believed she felt the same way, judging by the look on her face. He was saved when the waitress came ambling along with their food. "I guess we'll have to indulge in the second greatest sensory delight first."

"Oh, God. What now?" she asked, with an exasperated look on her face.

"What?" he asked, the innocent man.

"Have you always been so intellectual? Okay, I'll bite. What's the second whatever you said?"

"Eating, like sex, is the only time you use all five of your senses. Drinking is kind of in the same league, but you really don't get much of the sense of hearing or even touching, like the other two."

"Eating and drinking? That is interesting."

"Yeah, and if you overindulge in either one, look what happens. You get fat or go alcoholic. Smoking could be close. It's interesting that all are extremely hard to get control of once you've crossed the line. Too many senses involved."

"Are you sure those are the only ones?"

"I don't know much about drugs, street or otherwise. Maybe when you sniff—"

"Snort."

"Yeah, snort coke. Maybe druggies get similar sensations."

"How do you come up with this stuff? Does it just pop into your head?"

"Sometimes. But mostly I read and then stare at blank walls. Sometimes I even stare through other people," he said staring directly at her cleavage again.

"Stop."

He looked back into her eyes. "No, really, I have no idea. The thoughts just come, and I listen."

"Just like me...and hopefully soon," she said, wiggling around. "God, I'm terrible. No seriously, that's a real gift. Let's get a room. Now."

They cut their meal short and drove to the Holiday Inn just down the street. It was dark outside when they checked in, this time just one room, just one bed. Jesse paid cash. It was getting very easy to forget why they were on this road trip in the first place. By the time he locked the Take-Us and brought up the last of the luggage, the bathroom door was closed. He could hear the shower running. He was tempted to go in, but fought down the temptation. Instead, he turned the television on and started watching WCN. The hourly update was on, but not much was happening. Nothing about the Take-Us. That had already played earlier. When he heard the water stop, he turned the set to an XM channel playing love songs and sat on the bed. No sense taking a chance.

It seemed like hours passed before the door opened and Leena came out and stood at the foot of the bed. Her hair was up in a towel and she had no makeup on. She was beautiful, just standing there with a big towel wrapped around her.

She slowly reached her hand up to the top of the towel. As she loosened it, she said in a low, husky voice, "What you see is what you get."

She unwrapped the towel slowly and Jesse's face fell when he realized she was wearing a short, black, silky nightie. She laughed out loud. "If you want to see more, Mr. Sleep-in-the-barn-man, go take a shower."

Jesse shot off the bed as if his ass was on fire. It was actually the other side that was on fire. He stripped off his T-shirt and threw it in the corner as he passed her and stopped for a quick kiss. He was in the bathroom in a heartbeat and took the world's fastest shower. Moving toward the door, he thought he heard muted voices. Leena must have turned on the television.

Jesse put on a pair of shorts under his towel, deciding to get back at her for her stunt. He pulled a comb through his reddish-blond hair, splashed a few drops of cologne on, and glanced one last time in the mirror.

He was ready.

He opened the bathroom door quickly and saw a man in a gray suit, holding a black leather briefcase in his right hand as if it was a gun. Leena had put on a sweatshirt and stood glaring at the man, her shapely legs uncovered.

The man stared at Jesse, contemplating him, and then looked back at Leena. "Aren't you going to introduce us?"

She stayed silent.

The man sighed. "I recognize you from the television, Mr. Christenson. My name is Bradford Givings," he said, speaking in that nasal, East Coast upper-crust way He never bothered putting out his hand.

Jesse looked at Leena. She had a wild expression on her face that he had never seen before.

"Who is this guy?" Jesse demanded.

"Brad and I used to be…involved. That was before I found out he had a wife and children. He's a lawyer."

Like that explained everything. Jesse looked back at Givings.

"Mr. Christenson," Givings said, "that was years ago. I'm here today to offer you a business proposition."

"How did you find us?" Jesse asked, feeling a fire start in his gut.

"I already asked that," Leena said. "While you were taking your nap in the car, I called my boss. I told him we'd be spending the night in Omaha. And Brad is best friends with my boss."

"Once I got here, it wasn't very hard to find you. That car sticks out like a sore thumb." Bradford Givings held out his free thumb as if he were hitching a ride.

"What do you want?" Jesse asked, beginning to get pissed off.

"Do you mind if I sit?" Givings asked. Without waiting for an answer, he headed to the small table by the window and placed the briefcase on it.

"Do you mind if I put a shirt on?" Jesse reached into his overnight bag and quickly put on a clean T-shirt. Then he reached in and pulled out his pistol.

"There's no need for that," Givings said as he opened the briefcase and turned it around so Jesse could see inside. "This is a legitimate business offer."

Seeing no gun, Jesse handed the pistol to Leena. She looked mad enough to shoot Givings for any reason.

"What's the deal?" Jesse asked as he ripped off the towel, revealing the shorts underneath. Leena's eyebrows raised as she handed him back the pistol.

"Right to it, then. Okay. We want to buy your invention. The offer is one hundred million dollars," Givings said. He coaxed a chair out from under the table and sat down heavily.

Jesse looked at Givings, targeting the man's eyes. "Why that amount?" he asked, wondering why it wasn't ninety-nine million or seventy-seven million, seven hundred seventy-seven thousand. That would surely be lucky...all those sevens. He placed the pistol on the table and joined Givings, sitting down cautiously.

"We have determined that the value of your invention at this time is exactly that," Givings said and then softened his tone. "That is a great amount of money, Jesse. It will solve all your problems and make your dreams come true." Givings glanced at the other end of the room.

"What do you know about my problems?" Jesse asked. The money would solve all his problems except the one he was trying to solve, he thought. Thirty pieces of silver for a soul...

Givings continued, ignoring the question. "If you were to take that money and deposit it in, say, your savings account at El Dorado Bank, and received just five percent interest per annum—"

So, they already know I have a savings account and the name of my bank, Jesse thought.

"—that would net you, say, five million a year in interest, or about thirteen thousand, seven hundred dollars each and every day." Givings pointed the gold pen that was delicately balanced between his tidy fingers at the sheet of paper lying in front of him.

Jesse asked the obvious. "What if it's a leap year?"

"Leap year? What? Well, I guess it would be about the same, more or less, with one more day earning interest." He peered down and tapped his high-dollar pen.

"Mr. Givings, did you go to Harvard?" Jesse asked, studying the lawyer's face and noticing that the smooth, slick ice had a few cracks in it.

Givings looked up from his notes. "Yes, I did. However, I am uncertain what that has to do with this transaction. This isn't about me."

"Which school?"

"Well, law. And I have an MBA in business," Givings added, just a little too proudly.

"Who is 'we'?"

"I'm sorry. I don't understand."

"You just said 'we' determined that my invention was worth a hundred mil. Who's 'we'?"

"I'm sorry. I can't tell you that."

"Sorry? Let me get this straight." Jesse reached onto the table and spun the pistol. It was still spinning when he said, "You want to write me a check for a hundred million, and I don't even get to know who's signing it? Maybe you're just a sorry lawyer."

Givings watched as the pistol slowly came to a stop, pointing neither toward nor away from him. He quietly exhaled. "It would come from my office."

That was lame, Jesse thought. Several long minutes passed. The only sound was their breathing, both of them trying to keep it deep and slow, not allowing panic to break the silence. The smell of perfume still hung in the air. Jesse looked up at the cheaply papered wall a few inches above Mr. Givings's head. He knew this game. The first person to speak loses, most of the time, unless of course, it's to attack. After all, he had bought used cars before, just not for a hundred mil.

Jesse had no intention of losing. "Mr. Givings, what's the interest at five percent on a billion dollars?" He placed his hands on the table, palms up.

Givings looked up and smiled, smelling blood. Now that the parameters had been set, it was just a matter of negotiating the price.

"Well, Jesse, I don't know how much the interest is, but our offer is less than that amount, and it's still a considerable fortune."

It was the way he said "Jesse" that struck Christenson. Every time he heard it said like that, he knew he was in trouble. He had served in Nam, where one of those little bastards had shot him. "Look out, Jesse!" his buddy had yelled, just before disintegrating into a pile of smoke and yuck. Jesse ended up coming home on a stretcher, unceremoniously carried out of the ass end of an Air Force C-141 Starlifter with a big red cross on its tail. He'd been "looking out" ever since.

"I went to a different school than you did," Jesse said, looking straight into Mr. Bradford Givings's dark, darting eyes. "The school I graduated from was the School of Rock Hard Unforgiving No-Bullshit, with a major in Gonna Screw You Before You Screw Me. My diploma was a Purple Heart. And somewhere along the way I learned that a billion is ten times more than a hundred million, and so the interest is ten times more—"

Mr. Givings started to interrupt him. Jesse raised his hand to silence him, and being a good little lawyer, Givings promptly shut up.

"I don't know who your 'we' is, but I can imagine. They know as I do that my invention, the Take-Us, will change the power structure of the world. Many companies that made a combined six hundred billion in profit last year will go broke. The powerful will become powerless, and wars that are ongoing now will fizzle out. However, I also know that I will be personally responsible for other wars starting and many, many thousands of people getting killed. I've had this invention in my thoughts for over twenty years, and I've thought through all the ramifications." Jesse noted the surprise, clearly evident, that broke across Givings's poker face. "I know that if you offered me a hundred billion dollars it would still be a great deal for your—what did you call them?—'we.'"

"Listen, Mr. Christenson...er, Jesse." Givings spoke quietly as if he was afraid to be overheard. "You might think that you know the extent of the 'we.' However, I don't think you have the slightest idea how wide and deep it goes. They could pony up a hundred billion and not even blink. Nevertheless, I think they might try to go the cheaper route and simply eliminate the problem. Why don't you just take the money and have a good life?"

"A threat?" Jesse subconsciously picked up the pistol, knowing it would boil down to this, like dark after light: inevitable.

"Take it as a warning," Givings said, blowing out a deep breath. "You're a zealot, you know. You with your crazy blue eyes, trying to change things. You'll probably just die."

"I've almost died many times." Hearing the echo of a thousand acrid souls, Jesse spoke in a voice so loud even the Evil One couldn't miss it. "Death doesn't scare me,"

He remembered how it was back in the beginning. It had always been living he had more trouble with. Jesse turned to Leena, trying to see into her heart. It had been such a long time since he'd wanted to live. He sat there for a few long seconds, trying to see the future, without saying anything. Then he stood up abruptly. "Nope, not interested."

"Jesse, if I may call you that, I know you're not a stupid man. If you're not out to get rich, then what is your plan?"

"Mr. Givings, Leena said you have children. Is that correct?"

"Two boys, two girls." He held up four fingers.

"Do you want to see them blackmailed the way we have been for the past seventy years? Do you want to see your boys fighting in the desert sands of who-knows-where or maybe in some jungle somewhere? Isn't it time for the American civilization to shoot upward again? We've tried for years to dumb ourselves down so the rest of the world can catch up or, worse yet, made deals that left us unprotected. I think it's time to get rid of the anchors we've tied to our asses."

"Great speech. You want to be a politician?"

"Not exactly," Leena answered for him as she took the pistol and headed toward the bed. She put the pistol on the nightstand, sat down on the bed, and leaned back on the pillows. "Maybe you should hear him out, Brad. Try listening with that little, bitty heart you have."

"I'm sincere when I say this," Jesse said. "It's not about the money. It's about making the world a better place, not by taking away something that belongs to the 'Forgotten Man' to give to some undeserving person, but by allowing most people to start reaching for the stars on their own once again."

"Look, if we're not fighting over oil," Givings said, running his fingers through his dark hair, "it'll be something else. Let's see, your invention uses batteries and lots of copper wire. Therefore, the next big thing will be lead and copper. There will always be war."

"There's plenty of both lead and copper. However, that's not the point. We will still need oil. It's just that the oil market is backward to all other markets, with the possible exception being the diamond market. In other markets, the customer is in control because he can take his money to a competitor and negotiate a better deal. Oil is different because they know you can't go anywhere else. It's a cooperative monopoly. Take away the demand and the price will drop like a stone in a bucket of water. My guess is your clients have already foreseen this."

"Yes, they have. Nevertheless, my clients are legitimate countries and corporations that knew something was coming many years ago and have been diversifying ever since. They don't necessarily want to stop you. They just want to be under the cloud when it bursts. They want to get wet, real wet."

They continued talking back and forth for several hours. Jesse looked at Leena at one point. She was curled up around a fat pillow, fast asleep.

Brad caught his glance. "I wanted to get a divorce and marry her. When she found out about my marriage, she said she would never break up a family. No matter how much I begged, she wouldn't budge. She dumped me."

"How long ago was that?"

"Almost seven years ago. I'm best friends with her boss so I can tell you—at least according to my friend—that she hasn't dated anyone since. I envy you." The lawyer made a sad grimace.

"You know, I would like to trust you, but I equate the words *pond scum* and *lawyer* as being the same."

Givings laughed. "Me, too, generally, but the next time you have to go to court, try filling a jar with pond scum and let me know your results. But seriously, listen. I don't think you have to give this Take-Us car idea away."

No wonder Leena had once loved this guy. Maybe they had more in common than he first thought. "I never said I was going to give it away."

Jesse covered Leena with a blanket. Once again, he reached into his bag and then walked back and handed over the business card from Richard DeMonroe of General Motors, Hybrid Division.

"They're interested."

The lawyer studied the card for a few quiet minutes. You could almost see him wrestling with himself. He tapped his gold pen on the desk. "This gives me an idea that could be good for you and for our whole country."

They continued to discuss it until after two in the morning, when Givings snapped his briefcase shut and stood to leave. They shook hands and agreed to meet in San Francisco in three days. The lawyer departed.

Jesse knelt over the bed and gently gave Leena a kiss on the cheek. She gave a short gasp, rolled over, and went back to sleep. He lay down next to her, his troubled mind moving at light speed. After awhile he fell asleep. Sometime in the middle of the night, he felt Leena lying against his back, spooning him. It felt perfectly natural.

Day Three

Chapter 16

The Danger Sign

The telephone on the nightstand rang.

Leena rolled over, leaned on top of Jesse, and fastened her lips securely on his.

The phone rang again.

She broke the kiss. "How was it?" she asked in a deep, sexy voice.

"How was what?" Jesse yawned.

The phone rang again.

"You mean I didn't sleep through it?" Before he could answer, Leena put her hand around his neck, pulled him to her again, and kissed him even more deeply.

The phone rang again.

"Okay, okay," she said and picked up the phone. "Yes?"

She sat straight up in bed, her bare breasts jutting out. Sometime in the night, she had taken off the sweatshirt and her nightie. She listened intently.

"All right!" She slammed the phone down and frantically climbed out of bed. "We have to leave right now! We're in danger!"

She turned and ran to the bathroom. "I'll make it up to you, I promise." She stopped and sashayed back. "I don't want to leave, either."

It was the first time he'd seen her naked. He tore his eyes off her body, one of the most difficult things he'd ever done. "What danger?" he asked in a voice he hardly recognized. "Who was that?"

"Brad. Givings. He told me they tracked us to Omaha."

"Who tracked us?" Jesse wondered fleetingly if the lawyer was screwing up his love life on purpose.

"Arabs, Iranians...terrorists for sure." She slipped into some white-lace, butt-floss underwear and hurried into the bathroom, bra in hand.

Jesse leaped out of bed when he heard "Arabs," and started putting his clothes on. "Terrorists. Damn. Anything else?"

"He told me Senator Charlton is dead."

"So what's that to us?"

"Brad said the senator was on the payroll of some militant branch of Islam and was asking questions, looking for information about you. He thinks those people killed him."

That put a real charge in Jesse's battery. They both rushed around the room gathering up their belongings at breakneck speed and raced down to the car. Jesse was carrying the pistol in his right hand underneath a sweatshirt, the one Leena had worn the night before. The safety was off, both the gun and him. Leena stayed by the front door while he trotted to the Take-Us.

Jesse carefully looked around the parking lot, which was ominously deserted this early in the morning. He dropped down and crawled under the car, meticulously looking for anything that resembled a bomb, and found nothing out of the ordinary. The driver's door didn't look booby-trapped. He very gingerly opened it. Nothing happened. He quickly inspected the inside of the car.

They were safe...for now.

He grasped the steering wheel in a death grip and slowly pushed the accelerator pedal down and nothing unexpected happened, like being reduced to micrometer-sized dust. Relief washed over him. He drove to the door of the motel before Leena came over, just in case.

Leena walked up to the driver's door. "Good job, Double-Oh Seven. But, you forgot to inspect the passenger door. Come on, get out. I'll slide over and look at it." Seeing his face she continued, "You can't expect to be an expert at everything."

Once they were settled, Jesse turned out of the parking lot to get to the Interstate. When he thought how easy it would be to kill him, and by extension, Leena, he was demoralized.

Leena broke in on his thoughts, her voice the voice of reason. "There's no one on our tail. Maybe we should stop up here at Mc-Donalds and get some coffee and breakfast to go. I have a feeling this is going to be a long day."

"Do you think that's safe?"

"If they were going to gun us down, wouldn't it have been easier for them in the deserted parking lot?"

Jesse turned into McDonalds and looked at Leena, who had the pistol cradled in her lap. "It's been a long time since I've had to live in this kind of world. Now it seems like I'm the one who has to play catch up."

The sun was still low in the sky this early in the morning, another cloudless spring day that had the promise of becoming very hot. Leena decided to do the update interview first thing, and started looking for a rest area once they got back on the road. It was a short drive of sixty miles, short in comparison to the remainder of the journey. They still had more than sixteen hundred miles to go.

The rest area was just north of Lincoln, Nebraska. Like most rest stops along heavily traveled Interstate highways, it buzzed with activity. The comings and goings resembled bees to a bee hive, only on a planetary scale, operating on some kind of hidden, complex schedule.

Once again they parked the Take-Us toward the end of the parking lot, in the most out-of-the-way spot they could find, so they could conduct the interview without interference.

It was really starting to sink in to Jesse that he had not been paying much attention to their security. He thought it was probably because of his infatuation with Leena. If he wasn't more careful going forward, his little head was going to get his big head blown off. He scoped out the rest area, this time with a soldier's eye. He saw a car pull up and a young boy jump out and run for the bathroom, the boy's parents getting out and stretching before they went the same direction. There was a truck driver walking back to his rig with a cup of coffee in his hand, passing an Asian couple sitting at a picnic table in front of their Buick. The couple glanced at him and Leena occasionally, understandable since Leena was being very meticulous about getting the camera set up. He scrutinized the rest area one last time. Everything looked normal to him.

"Good morning, this is Leena Delaney, 'On the Road' once again with the fabulous Take-Us automobile." She spoke into the microphone held between the thumb and fingers of her right hand. "We've now traveled almost thirteen hundred miles without stopping for gas or, in this case, charging. Today, Jesse Christenson, the creator of the Take-Us, would like to tell you about one more of the additional benefits of this amazing automobile."

"Yes, Leena, the last time we spoke, I told you it really is a self-contained generating unit. When the rear wheels turn, it generates its own electrical power. It has the potential capability of changing the way we live our lives at home as well as on the road."

"How is that possible?"

"Imagine that when you come home from work, you drive into your garage and raise the back wheels of the car off the ground—easily done with the built-in hydraulic jacks, similar to those now in use on motor homes and fifth-wheel trailers. Then simply plug the Take-Us into your home. One of the electrical leads would go to your computer, which would monitor your home's electrical needs. That would communicate with the car's onboard computer to deliver the correct amount of energy your home requires. I also envision in the future that many of the Take-Us components will be water-cooled, and the hot water could be piped throughout the house for heating purposes."

While they were filming, a motor home left the rest area. The driver blew his horn. His partner stuck her arm out the open passenger window and waved to them as they went motoring past.

Leena filmed the motor home and Jesse said, "With the future, more advanced Take-Us system, that motor home could be self-sustaining. It could park for months at a time without being hooked up to an external electrical power source."

Leena said, "This is a true paradigm shift. After this, the standards will all change. Is that correct?"

"Well, we've traveled almost halfway across this great country of ours without refueling or having any problems with the vehicle. But this first version of Take-Us technology is equal to the Model T cars of the past. The Take-Us is just in its infancy. Maybe a better analogy would be the very first home computers. They were stationary. Now laptops and notebook computers are common. We've got all kinds of portable devices in our lives. This will soon give us our own portable, electric power plant."

"Is this then the answer to the elusive perpetual motion machine?"

"No way. This is just a machine that can overcome friction for a limited amount of time. Like all machines, it will wear out, and various parts will need to be replaced on an on-going maintenance schedule." Jesse took a step towards the camera and looked into the lens. "This is real, not some hokey, sci-fi theory."

Leena once again signed off and promised an update the next day. Being the VP of network programming, she had decided to air the update segments from the road for only one minute each day.

She pushed the transmit button and waited until a light went out before beginning the process of removing the camera from the tripod.

"Does this camera have GPS built in that tells our position to the receiving computer?" he asked, coming over to offer her a hand.

"Yes, I believe it does, but it's in latitude and longitude coordinates. You would have to run it through another program to decipher where the camera is actually located. Of course, if you're knowledgeable, you might be able to do it with a very precise map."

"So someone could find out where we are from this camera's signals?"

"Yes, I suppose so. But that someone would have to be at the incoming computer when the transmission downloaded." She wrinkled her brow. "You don't think they're tracking us by the camera, do you?"

"Not really. It has to be turned on and it needs a clear shot at the satellite. The signal couldn't go through the roof of that old barn, so it's probably not possible to go through the solid trunk lid of the car. No, I don't think they can track us that way, but after you transmit they could tell where we'd been."

"Why did you ask, then?"

"In case we wanted to be found—"

"Like in an emergency."

"Something like that," he said, changing the subject. "We need to stop somewhere to disguise the car. If Givings could find us that easily, others can, too. The next exit, we'll look for a good place."

They exited the Interstate, and turned into a spot next to a gently flowing river. Thick bushes and trees hid them from view of any unwanted prying eyes. They took the items that Leena had bought at the Wal-Mart in Illinois out of the trunk. Jesse started applying the car wax while Leena, using masking tape and brown paper, covered the windows and chrome.

"Where did you learn this?" she asked, putting on another strip of masking tape.

Jesse was bent over the car making small, swirling circles. "A buddy of mine who works at a body shop told me they do it when applying racing stripes. It's supposed to keep the over-spray from sticking to the paint, and we can wash it off at a car wash with a sprayer. The key is not to buff the wax after we apply it. The paint job won't look too good, but from a distance most people probably won't be able to tell the difference. It doesn't really matter. The paint only has to last for two days, and then we'll be home safe."

When they had the car prepped, Jesse spray-painted it the nice yellow Leena had bought. He hadn't given her any directions about any specific color. Then they removed the tape and stood back to marvel at what they'd accomplished.

"It sure looks a lot different." Leena wrinkled her nose.

"Different is good," Jesse said, remembering the lawyer's warning. "I just hope it buys us a little time."

"What about the license plate? You don't see very many California plates this far east."

"Yeah, but if you don't count speeding, we really haven't broken any laws. I'm not about to steal someone's license plate now."

"What about leaving the scene of a crime, crossing state lines to avoid prosecution, assault and battery—"

"He tried to shoot me, for Christ's sake! That's on him. But I'm no thief."

"You certainly have a selective sense of moral objectivity where you're concerned."

"People steal to make their lives easier, and that makes someone else's life harder. That's not morally right. Ever. I'm no thief," Jesse said crossing his arms.

She smiled, not saying a word.

They traced their way back to the Interstate. After a while the tension subsided, and once again they felt the exhilaration of freedom that is special to the open road. It wasn't long before they'd put hundreds of miles behind them. They stopped at North Platte, Nebraska, for a couple of sandwiches from the local Subway. When they left town Jesse saw the same Asian couple that had been at the rest stop that morning.

"They certainly aren't in any great hurry," he said, pointing.

"Who?" Leena looked around.

"Those people getting gas in the white Buick."

"Where did you see them?"

"They were at the rest stop this morning. I've noticed this… phenomenon…before when I've traveled. You can pass the same car two or three times during the day, almost like you're temporary companions on the road of life."

She nodded and gave him a sweet look. "Is that it?"

"What do you mean?" he asked, turning the Take-Us onto the ramp to get back on Interstate 80.

"Well, I've noticed that once you get on a roll philosophically, it's usually a long dissertation."

"I do ramble once in a while, huh?" he mumbled, looking over as a dirty, black Toyota Camry carrying three dark-complexioned men passed them. All three men stared at them.

The hair on the back of Jesse's neck stood up as straight as a young Marine at boot camp. He sneaked a glance at Leena. She'd seen the same thing.

Her voice was low and subdued. "Those guys give me a creepy feeling. Something about the way they stared at us, like they recognized us or something."

"Maybe they saw us on TV. I'm going to get off at the next exit." The sick feeling of fear started to boil in his stomach.

"I'll look at the Atlas and find us a different route," she said, her tone tense, tight.

The next exit was twelve or thirteen miles away, and Jesse could just barely see the Toyota way out in front of them. They turned briskly off the Interstate onto a wide country road. Then he took a deep breath, put his right foot down, and sped up to put as much distance as he could between the Interstate and them. He continued speeding along and was just starting to settle back into a comfortable routine when he saw flashing red lights in the rearview mirror.

"Damn! A cop." Jesse immediately slowed down to the speed limit.

"He couldn't get us for speeding. He's way too far behind us for his radar to work," Leena turned around in her seat and looked back. "Maybe he's on his way to an accident."

Jesse remained quiet for the few minutes it took the cop to catch up to them. He pulled slowly off to the side of the road. It seemed to have a wide shoulder. He was not surprised when the cop pulled in behind them.

"Oh, well," he said, rolling down the window.

Two Nebraska state troopers emerged from the cruiser. One walked up to his door and the other placed himself just behind the passenger door with his gun drawn. Jesse looked in the rearview mirror and saw a third man, dressed in a blue windbreaker with the letters FBI on it, standing behind the open rear door of the troopers' car. That's weird, he thought, and held his driver's license in his hand as he turned to greet the cop.

"Good afternoon, Officer." Jesse knew the drill, having gone through this routine more than a few times in his life.

"Please exit your vehicle," the trooper ordered.

Exit your vehicle? Who speaks that way, Jesse thought as the trooper opened the door.

"You, too," the trooper said to Leena.

"I haven't done anything," she said, and as an afterthought, added, "I'm a member of the press. I report for WCN." Her voice had a hard tone to it.

"We know who you are," the man said. "Get out."

His partner aggressively swung open her door.

As he was getting out of the car, Jesse figured the deputy sheriff in Indiana must have finally reported them. He then noticed that this cop looked like an Arab, too. He glanced across the top of the car to the trooper's partner, who was also dark. Jesse slowed his step, reaching the rear of the Take-Us where the cop indicated he should put his hands on the trunk.

At that moment everyone's attention was diverted by another vehicle pulling in behind the police cruiser, creating a small cloud of dust. It was the white Buick.

The Asian man and his wife emerged from the car. The man had a map unfolded in his hands and said something in Chinese, or at least it sounded Asian. He started walking toward the troopers. "Preeze...I, we loss...You help, yes?" he asked, moving his head up and down in the affirmative.

"You! Stay where you are," the trooper at the driver's door ordered. His gun hand dropped to his holster.

The Asian man stopped four feet away. He abruptly dropped the map and in his hand was a pistol. BOOM! The first shot struck the trooper in the center of his chest, knocking him backward. BOOM! The second shot tore into his throat and sent the trooper slamming to the ground. Blood spurted everywhere. The Asian gunman then raced deliberately to the other side of car. There was a flurry of shooting. BOOM! BOOM!

Jesse reacted quickly when the shooter moved off. He reached down and pulled the trooper's pistol out of its holster. He heard more shooting behind him and on the other side of the car. He knelt behind the car and was aiming the gun across the trunk when he heard Leena's scream.

That was it. He didn't care anymore. He practically jumped to the other side of the car, thumbing back the hammer on the pistol. When he got there, both the gunman and the other trooper were down. He slowly released and reset the hammer. Leena had blood on her face. She pointed backward when she saw him. He had forgotten about the man in the FBI jacket. Jesse jerked around, raising the pistol, but the man in the blue windbreaker was also down. So was the Asian woman from the Buick. How did—? He didn't care. He rushed to Leena's side.

"Where are you hit?" He touched her face, looking for the source of her wound.

"It's theirs," she said when she saw the blood on his fingers. "I'm okay. Are you?"

Before he could answer, they heard a voice.

"You must leave at once. There are more on the way." The Asian man spoke in perfect English. "Please help me up."

"Who are you?" Jesse asked, cocking the hammer back with a resounding, sharp click and pointed his newly acquired pistol at the Asian man's chest.

After seeing the pistol, the man said, "My name is Jaeho. But that is not important. You are being tracked…There is a GPS tracking device hidden somewhere on your car."

"How do you know that?"

"How do you think we found you? There is a service, like OnStar, that will trace you anywhere. For the right price…in America… everything is for sale." His breath came in short gasps.

"Who are they?" Jesse asked, nodding toward the dark-complexioned men, but not moving the pistol from Jaeho's chest.

He said something in Chinese and then remembered, almost spitting it out. "Islamic terrorists from Iran."

"Help him up," Leena said from behind. "I believe him."

Jesse checked to make sure Jaeho didn't have a gun in his hand before he released the hammer and lowered the pistol. He reached down and pulled Jaeho to his feet, which drew a small, involuntary cry from his lips. After Jaeho was standing, he reached his hand down and touched the blood coming out of the hole in his shirt just below stomach level. The blood was black. Jaeho looked up into Jesse's eyes and nodded. They both knew it was a death sentence.

"He has body armor on. That's how he got me," Jaeho said, looking down at the body of the second trooper. There were two bullets holes in the front of his shirt, and one in the center of his forehead. The back of the trooper's head was missing.

Jaeho started to shuffle toward the troopers' car behind them. Jesse and Leena followed. Jaeho stopped at the door and looked down at the body on the ground. The man with the FBI jacket was lying on his side and had been shot at least half a dozen times. Like the others, he also had body armor, and the fatal shot looked like it entered his left eye. He still had his gun in one hand and a cell phone in the other. Jesse kicked the gun out of his hand and under the car.

"Is he really an FBI agent?" Leena asked.

"Yes. We must hurry," Jaeho said, starting to walk away.

"Are they real troopers, too?" she asked, not moving.

The man nodded. "Yes." He continued walking until he'd reached the woman lying on the blood-soaked ground. He bent down and touched her face. "Oh, Janae."

He hesitated before slowly straightening up. "Could you please put her in the car for me?" he asked, struggling to keep the sadness from his voice. "In the front seat," he said when Jesse started to open the back door.

Jesse handed the pistol to Leena and bent down to pick up the woman's body. She was surprisingly light. He slid her onto the front seat as requested.

Jaeho opened the back door of the car, reached in, and brought out an M16 with iron sights. "Here, take this." He handed Jesse the rifle.

Jesse pulled the magazine out. It was full.

"There's already one in the chamber," Jaeho said and struggled to hand him a heavy green bag. "Inside you will find a bandoleer of extra clips and some other weapons you might find useful." Jaeho gave him a wry smile. "I am sure you will remember how to use them…Sergeant."

"Who are you?" Jesse asked once again.

Ignoring the question, Jaeho said, "They are slow, but not stupid. By now they also know much about you."

"Who are you?"

Jaeho reached down with his fingers and touched the blood that was soaking his shirt. It was obvious he was weighing what he was about to say, and something inside reached the tipping point.

"I am from China, an agent for my government. She, also." He looked tenderly at the dead woman next to him. "It is important to my people as well as your own that the Take-Us car be produced. I have saved your lives," he said as he put his hand up and paused to cough. His hand came away with blood on it. "And I want you to promise me you will make the car available to my country."

Without hesitation, Jesse said, "I will promise that." He reached out to take Jaeho's hand. It felt deathly cold.

Leena also reached for his hand and then changed her mind and gave him a hug instead. It caused him to let out a small gasp. "Thank you for our lives," she said.

"You must go. Now. Trust no one. Stay on the main highway… safer. Wait and follow me back to the Interstate…stay more than a kilo…more than a half mile behind me."

Jesse squinted, the afternoon sun bright in his eyes as he looked in both directions at the almost imperceptible curves of the deserted country road. "All right, we'll stay back at least a half mile."

"One more thing," Jaeho said as his face softened and then creased into pain as he coughed up another bit of bloody spit. "According to our traditions…please"—another cough—"have our remains returned home…to China."

***

Jesse had lost track of how many miles they were from the Interstate, but figured it must be between twenty and thirty. They were following behind the Buick at least a half mile, maybe a little more. The Chinese agent was in a hurry, going well over eighty miles per hour. Jesse started to understand how bad an idea it had been to get off the Interstate. They hadn't passed another car in all the time they'd been on this road.

"I knew those cops couldn't be legit," Leena blurted out.

"How? I caught on that you were suspicious."

"When they approached the car they were ready for action. That meant they were looking for us."

"So?"

"We're not in a red car anymore. How in the hell did they know we were in a yellow car?"

Both of them stared straight ahead through the windshield, trying hard to think, still shaken by their lucky escape. He could see another car approaching, but it was still too far away to tell if it was another police car.

"So what do you think? How did they know we painted the car?" he asked.

"I don't know. Yet. I'm working on it." Leena frowned intently.

The approaching auto closed the distance fast. It was just in front of the Buick when the Chinese agent suddenly swerved directly into its path. There was no time for the other driver to react, and the two cars collided head on with incredible fury at a combined speed of 160 miles per hour.

Leena screamed, "Dear God!"

Jesse slammed on the brakes.

A huge fireball, towering at least fifty feet, exploded from one of the vehicles. The white Buick stayed on its wheels, but the flaming car flipped over. In a last gasp, one of the front tires popped feebly off and rolled, wobbling, into a field next to the road. Pieces, parts, and debris rained down, scattering over both lanes of the highway.

The Take-Us stopped well before the crash site, shrouded now in dust and smoke. The Buick had come to rest in a ditch next to a fence. Jesse got out and approached the car. There was little left of it. The entire front end and engine had smashed into one ugly unit. He could see body parts and blood splattered all over the inside of the car. When he looked at the Chinese agent, there was no doubt. His neck had a huge gash across it, and his head was barely attached. He was as dead as yesterday. The woman's body was unrecognizable.

Jesse started to gag, then turned away and approached the other car. It was on fire in the middle of the road. He was having a difficult time figuring out just what type of car it was. There were two bodies in the front seat and both were on fire. He was just about to brave the flames and try to get them out when Leena called out, "Jesse! Over here."

She was on the other side of the road and there was a third man, who must have been ejected from the car. His body was impaled on a metal fence post. The barbed wire kept him from sliding the rest of the way to the ground. The man was way past dead. He had on a blue windbreaker, similar to the third man at the first scene, except this one had ATF written in large letters on the back of it.

Leena stared at the man. Jesse got down on one knee and looked up at him. "Alcohol, Tobacco, and Firearms. Another dark-complexioned man."

Jesse turned back around and studied the car. It was a dark color: black or maybe dark blue. He inspected it more closely and could see, now that he knew what he was looking for, that it was a Toyota Camry. "That's the car that passed us on the Interstate."

"With the three men in it," Leena said. "I knew there was something not quite right about them."

"Let's get out of here." Jesse stared down the roadway, putting his hand up to shade his eyes. But all he could see were the hot mirage waves coming off the scalding blacktop. "Hurry," he added and when she broke into a run, he followed closely in her slipstream.

Jesse drove carefully around the debris spread around everywhere. The last thing they needed right now was a flat tire. When they were abreast of the impaled body, he suddenly stopped the car. "Where is the dead trooper's gun?"

"Here. On the floor by my feet."

"Can I have it? I have an idea." Jesse reached under the seat and took out the blue shop towel and wiped the gun clean of their fingerprints. Then he jogged over, and placed it next to the dead agent's body.

"I get it. You used that same shop towel in Indiana. If they look close enough they'll see the connection between all three crime scenes," Leena said, a subdued quality to her voice. "That's smart."

"It's the only smart thing I've done today," he said, shaking his head and thinking it was just way too simple to get themselves killed.

Since the road was flat and straight, Jesse sped up to more than a hundred miles per hour and got back to the Interstate in no time. Once on the highway, it was extremely difficult to hold his speed below eighty.

"Remember what the Chinese agent said?" Leena suddenly said.

"Which part?"

"We have a transmitter attached somewhere. They're still tracking us."

"Shit! In all the excitement, I forgot," he said, thinking hard and fast. "I looked at everything under the car this morning. Then at the rest stop, I checked out the trunk. I didn't see anything strange in there."

Leena opened the glove box, took everything out, and looked in there. She jammed it all back in. "Nothing here."

She got down on her knees and looked under the seat, her hands darting everywhere. "I don't even know what the fuck I'm looking for," she shouted, as tears started to run down her cheeks, "Do you?"

"Not exactly. But wait a minute. Wait!" he commanded. That certainly caught her attention. He forced himself to cool down. In a much calmer voice, he said, "Your mom's new car came equipped with OnStar, didn't it?"

Leena nodded.

"I thought I saw a small antenna on top of the car," he said.

"Yes, a black one."

"And your camera in the trunk. It has to be somewhere outside with a clear view of the sky to transmit. Correct?"

She nodded, starting to follow his logic. "So, since there is no antenna on top of this car, the device has to be somewhere in plain sight. Is that what you're saying?"

"Absolutely."

They both looked around and spotted it at the same time. Leena climbed into the back seat and reached into the back window for their driving mascot: the stuffed tiger.

She turned it over. "There's a slit in the bottom of his guts." She stuck her fingers inside and pulled out a small, black rectangle, measuring about two inches by three. She held it up for him to see.

"That little bastard!" Jesse yelled.

"Who?"

"Fatah or Fasil, something like that. He was holding it when I gave those guys from General Motors a ride. That prick!"

"You think he's a terrorist?"

"I don't know," Jesse said, trying to sort it out. "What did the Chinese agent say about everything in America being for sale? Maybe GM wants to stop us, too."

Leena climbed back into the front seat and started to roll her window down.

"Wait! Put it up on the front dash," Jesse ordered.

"But it will tell them where we are," she said, much calmer now.

"They, whoever the hell they are, already know. However, less than fifty miles ahead, Interstate 80 splits and Interstate 76 goes to Denver. If we were avoiding trouble, it would be logical that we'd turn off and take a different route. Let's go one exit that way. Maybe the GPS tracking unit can hitch a little ride to Denver."

"Great idea, Double-Oh Seven." A police car went screaming by in the opposite direction. "We also need to change the color of the car again. And by the way, you need to change your tone of voice when speaking to me," she said with just the smallest of smiles creeping to her lips.

It didn't work often, but sometimes the instructions passed down through his genes from one man to another kicked into gear. He shut up.

They drove by Ogallala, Nebraska, and in a short time took the split onto Interstate 76 toward Denver. Jesse spotted the exit and turned into a truck stop. They parked among the eighteen-wheelers. Leena stayed with the Take-Us while Jesse meandered through the parking lot until he spotted the perfect truck for their purposes: a flatbed with cargo strapped under a tarp. Looking around and not seeing anybody, he climbed up onto trailer and stuffed the tiger securely into a small valley on top of some kind of John Deere farm machinery. It had a clear view of the sky.

He was just rounding the last tractor-trailer on his way back when he saw a small crowd gathered around Leena. She was gesturing and talking excitedly to them.

"There he is now," she said, pointing. "The inventor of the Take-Us car."

One of the drivers, a big beefy man, stuck his callused hand out. "Mr. Christenson, this is a real pleasure for me. Will this automobile really change the way things are? Like ya said on TV?" he asked in a deep voice with a Southern accent

"Everything I said on TV is true. This car, or rather the technology behind it, is the future."

"Lordy be, with the fuel prices what they are, it's what's causin' so much pain in this country," he said as the other truckers gathered around and started shaking Jesse's hand.

"Jesse," Leena said, "I was just explaining that we were having a small problem with so many cars pulling up next to us, waving and taking pictures. I told them how we've almost been run off the road at least a dozen times. All of these nice people have volunteered to help us change the color one more time."

"That's great," Jesse said with what he hoped sounded like a laugh in his voice. "But we'll have to swear everybody to secrecy."

Leena had the paper and tape out. She soon started directing people and had the car masked off in minutes. Jesse went into the store and bought some cans of black spray paint. With everyone's help, the whole process took less than an hour from the time they exited the Interstate. Leena and Jesse stood back and looked at the car and then each other. They were both so relieved they burst into laughter.

A lady truck driver, wife of the big trucker who'd spoken to Jesse earlier, walked up to them and said, "You can tell y'all have some kinda chemistry goin' on. I saw it clear as day on TV."

Leena put her finger over her lips and whispered, "That's supposed to be a secret."

"Honey, if I could tell, so can every other woman in America. Maybe even half the men, if they can stop starin' at your tits long enough."

Jesse choked down a laugh and walked off to talk with the men, hiding his smile and leaving the two women to banter.

When he finally got Leena off to the side and out of earshot, Jesse whispered, "Maybe we should go into the store and stock up on supplies while we're here. There are probably more you-know-whos on the way. I think we might need to make a run for it."

Leena straightened up and looked over at the people clustered around the Take-Us. "Look at all these people; check out their expressions. The terrorists may kill us, but they will never steal our dreams. Those people believe in you."

He could feel the long-buried Sergeant Christenson starting to awaken. Kill us, maybe, he thought, but not easily and not without a fight.

Chapter 17

The Evil Darkens

It was four in the morning when Rashid Marashi tapped lightly on the colonel's door, awakening him. The colonel had a couch in his office and spent many nights like this.

"Yes. What is it?" the colonel asked, aware of his arid sore throat and hoarse voice.

"Colonel Mafsanjani. Sir. You said to alert you if any news came in about the American state, Nebraska."

"Yes?" His dark, tired eyes burrowed straight into his underling.

"The American news reports a very large auto crash, killing at least eight people. Two were paramilitary, called...troopers."

"Fucking Americans. Bring me the tapes. And coffee." Mafsanjani thought of the many cups of coffee he had spiked over the many long years. "Wait. I will make my own coffee." He dug into his desk drawer, grabbed a cigarette, and lit it.

Marashi scurried away as quickly as possible, leaving the door slightly ajar. He had served Colonel Mafsanjani for many years. The colonel was known to shoot people when he was pissed.

The smell of cigarette smoke and coffee soon filled Mafsanjani's office. What time was it in America right now, he wondered, still groggy from lack of sleep. The American state of Nebraska was somewhere in the middle, so it must be early evening, after six o'clock. Oh, Allah, what a day it had been. The ill-fated death of Senator Charlton, as if any infidel's death could be a bad thing, was just bad timing. He'd been expensive. But his information, although spotty lately, had been first class. They didn't have anyone else with his level of contacts, something Mafsanjani would have to correct. All it took was money. One of his sleeper agents in their Homeland Security Department reported that Charlton had died of drugs mixed with alcohol. The American news stations said it was a heart attack. He believed his agent. She also reported there was a rumor about a deputy sheriff in Indiana mixed up with terrorists. It was just something she heard; there were no details as of yet.

Marashi returned, bringing two news videos—one of them about the accident—and a sheaf of papers. He waited nervously while the colonel reviewed the first video. It was generic: no pictures, just a promise to get back to the story once more details emerged. Marashi had also brought the news update on the Take-Us automobile, which coincidentally followed the report of the accident.

"It would appear that both units were lost," the colonel said, filling his cup with deep-dark coffee. "But at least they managed to stop the car and eliminate them both. The woman's report must have been recorded earlier."

"Sir," the underling said, swallowing hard "the, um…"

"Yes, go ahead. Speak."

"We have a report from unit three. The tracking device planted on the car is now on their Interstate 76"—Marashi took a deep, tense breath—"heading in the direction of the city of Denver, in their state of Colorado."

The colonel did not speak. He took a long swallow of his coffee, the papers he held in his hand shaking like leaves in the wind. Peering directly at his underling, he asked, "Could there be a mistake? I was told they would take Interstate 80 all the way to San Francisco."

"We thought that could be so, but when our people handling the GPS checked again, it was the same result. Unit one reported that Christenson changed the color of the car to yellow. And we now have unit three on the way to Denver. They will be looking for the car."

"Is Denver on the way to San Francisco?"

"It appears on the map that the highway splits and it is an equal distance either way."

"Let us look at that tape again."

"Yes, sir."

"See here, the car is still red in this report. Therefore, it has to be a taped interview. The fool still never bothered to change the license plate. Wait, back that up. Let me see the woman's face again." The colonel stared intently, replaying the tape several times. "I did not notice it before, but there is the look of love that shows when she speaks to the man. What do we know of this woman?"

"I do not know, sir." Marashi thought it unwise to know too many secrets around here. "We keep an extensive record of all foreign reporters. Most are spies."

"Yes, I know, fool."

"I will get on it right away, sir."

"Go, then."

The underling spun on his heel and disappeared, closing the door softly. He could not believe his luck. He was useful, and therefore still alive. Bearers of unpleasant news had a short life expectancy around the colonel.

Alone now in his office, the colonel patiently watched the interview many more times. Patience was the most necessary requirement of a good intelligence officer. Look for the small details, he told himself. That was how he'd spotted the license plate in the first place and traced it to this Jesse Christenson of California.

Earlier that night, President Ahmadinejad had called for an operational update. The Little Nib had spoken with great knowledge about the drive system of this Take-Us car. Apparently, someone from OPEC had filled him in; he was too lazy to do his own research. The colonel agreed with the president's assessment that this would do their country great harm if not stopped. The rabid Little Nib had somehow gathered the courage to remind Mafsanjani, once again, that the price for failure would be his neck stretched out on the chopping block.

Mafsanjani laughed. He had many powerful friends, many coerced—just like the Quran taught—because of the extensive files he had gathered on each. It would not be his neck that was stretched.

He took a sip of his dark, bitter coffee. The plan to get this man

Christenson to sign an agreement to sell them the legal rights and then kill him must be modified. If Christenson could eliminate two complete units plus one solo assassin, he must have very good skills. His file indicated he was a decorated veteran, a paratrooper who had served with the elite 101st Airborne Division in the war in Vietnam. The other units needed to be warned about how dangerous this man Christenson was and to take appropriate precautions. He would authorize them immediately to use any means necessary to kill Christenson and destroy the car.

The soft tap at his door brought Mafsanjani out of his reverie. "Enter."

"I have the file on the woman."

"Go ahead."

"The woman's real first name is Kaikalina. She is not an active reporter anymore. She was promoted to senior vice president of programming with WCN. She attended college in California and apparently grew up in the same village the man Christenson lives in. We checked on the Internet and found a woman named Malie Delaney, who lives on the same street as Christenson."

"Malie and what? Kaikalina? Unusual names for Americans."

"We thought as much and checked. The names are from the island of Hawaii that the Americans conquered," Marashi said and then smiled. He looked like a dog waiting for a bone.

"Probably the mother lived there at one time. Contact unit four and have them go to the mother's house. They can make up some excuse to stay there. Wait. I will deal with this myself. Leave the file. You are dismissed."

Chapter 18

DHS—The Filth Abounds

It was a few minutes after six in the evening in Washington, D.C. Once again Patrick O'Hallohan had assumed control of the night duty officer's position. His usual position at Homeland Security was not that much different from the one he'd held in the Army. He was in charge of the Rapid Response Team (RRT), which was organized on the same lines as the Delta teams he'd commanded. The major difference was that Homeland Security was civilian-controlled and only for use in the sovereign United States. He didn't wear a uniform in the office, but almost all the agents in DHS had served in some branch of the military. Of course, there were also many active military personnel assigned there, TDY, ever since the war started. One of the men, a Marine Corps sergeant, marched up to him and announced, "There's a call for you, sir."

O'Hallohan walked briskly to the closest desk, sat down, and reached for the phone. "This is Duty Officer Patrick O'Hallohan. How may I be of assistance?"

"This is Mike Nowiki, FBI. I'm on a secure satellite phone."

The name was slightly familiar to O'Hallohan. "What's up, Agent Nowiki?"

"How about eight dead bodies? One FBI agent, two Nebraska state troopers, an ATF agent, an employee of the IRS, and a postal employee...all of Middle-Eastern descent."

"FBI agent and what? A mailman? And Arabs? Hang on a second. I want to get this recorded." Most of the staff in the room had heard his outburst and were staring at O'Hallohan. He realized he was standing up. "Hold on, I need to get to my office."

Once there, O'Hallohan sat down at the computer and keyed the voice recognition software to record and simultaneously display a transcript on his computer screen.

"State your name and position once again, please."

"Special Agent Mike Nowiki, FBI. I guess you'll know it's really me when I call from now on, huh?"

"Something like that. You were saying you had a dead FBI agent and..."

"Eight bodies: one agent, two Nebraska state troopers, an ATF agent, an IRS guy, and a fellow who's a post office employee."

"Arabs?"

"Middle-Eastern descent."

Patrick sat looking at the monitor as the words appeared on the screen. "I only count six. You said eight."

"The other two are Asians: a male and a female. Both appear to have been shot before getting into an auto accident."

"Where did this happen?"

"Nebraska, near North Platte. Way out in the boonies."

"Is this the auto accident that was on the news?"

"The auto accident was part of it. We're using the accident for cover from the media. There appear to be two separate crime scenes about ten miles apart. The other was a big-time shootout. They're connected, but we're not exactly sure how."

"Tell me about the Arabs, uh, Middle Eastern men?"

"Are you familiar with an incident that happened in Indiana yesterday?"

"Nowiki. That's where I saw your name." Patrick jotted down his name on a piece of paper and circled it.

"Yeah, I'm the lead agent on that case, too. That's why they sent me here."

"Indiana. You're talking about that deputy sheriff. Is he still unconscious?"

"He's in a medically induced coma, but I have a feeling they'll be waking him real soon."

"So what's the connection?"

"The FBI agent and the two staties were killed in the shootout on a rural road. It looks like a routine traffic stop. The problem is, both troopers were off duty, and the agent had called in sick. When we searched the cruiser they were riding in, we found laptop computers and multiple passports. Just like the deputy in Indiana."

"Holy shit. What about the other three?"

"The car they were in blew up at the time of the accident. Two of the bodies were badly burned. The third was ejected, but impaled on a fence post."

"Ouch."

"Really. Next to his body, we found a pistol that belonged to one of the dead troopers, which is weird because it had never been fired. That's how we know the two events are connected. We also found a laptop about fifty feet from the crashed vehicle. The fire burned up most of the other stuff. We have an evidence team en route and if there were passports, we'll find them."

"Two three-man teams," Patrick said, thinking aloud. "Three-man teams would be consistent with an Iranian or Hezbollah cell, according to what we've gleaned since 9/11."

"Right. Do you have any information you can share about the threat level issued by your office?"

"The NSA, along with many of the other branches sharing information with us, picked up chatter. It emanated from a lot of places: Iran, Venezuela, Russia—hey, you said you have some dead Asians. Could they be Chinese?"

"Could be. All I know is that they're Asian. They caused the traffic accident, according to the troopers who first arrived on the scene. Why?"

"The NSA also picked up chatter from China. It didn't make any sense then, and it still doesn't. I know it's too early to figure out exactly what happened out there, but do you have any kind of gut feeling?"

"The incident in Indiana and the one out here are connected. I don't know how, yet. But more importantly, and it doesn't take a rocket scientist to figure this out, we're being systematically penetrated."

Patrick wrote SPY. FBI and ATF. DHS, too? Then he crossed it off, and wrote SPIES plural, instead. "Get the names of the dead inputted as soon as possible and send it my way. Send it to me 'Eyes Only.' I'll begin the backgrounds."

"It's being done as we speak."

"Nowiki, one more thing. Try to keep this under wraps as much as possible."

The deep sigh didn't register on the computer screen but Patrick heard it just the same. "Yeah, I already put that together. Might be a week or so for me to finalize my report. That enough time?"

"I'll get back to you."

Patrick terminated the call and saved the information in a secure file that only he and Deputy Director Gustoffson could access. Having worked in the field most of his career, O'Hallohan had never been an office weenie and had no idea what the procedure was to report a breach of security, which he now thought was a high probability. Normally he'd go to his immediate supervisor, Deputy Director Gustoffson. But what did he really know about Gustoffson, except that the man had hired him? As a matter of fact, what did he know about the Secretary of DHS? Oh man, this was getting too weird.

What an incredibly difficult decision to make. If he blew it, he might set back any attempt of ever catching—wait a minute. Gustoffson was with the Secretary of Homeland Security, who was doing an interview with WCN at this moment. They couldn't both be dirty, could they? This new information was so hot he didn't think it should be left until morning. The Secretary always had a secure phone, carried at all times by his bodyguard.

"This is DHS Night Duty Officer Patrick O'Hallohan. I have some extremely important information that just came in. The Secretary needs to hear it."

"Is this an emergency?" the voice on the other end of the phone asked.

"No, not in an urgent life-or-death sense, but it's pretty damned important," Patrick said, and thought, why do you think I fuckin' called, asshole?

"The Secretary is in the middle of an interview at the present time. I will relay your message. You can expect a call back soon."

Patrick slowly returned the headset to its place, his brain afire.

Since the terrorist attacks of 9/11, many smaller bureaucracies had been reorganized into the giant, new Department of Homeland Security. One of its primary missions was to start building a database on every person—citizen or not—who lived in America. The computers at Homeland Security were some of the most powerful in the world. "Information equals power" had always been true and always would be. The government under President Roosevelt interned thousands of Japanese Americans during World War II. It might have stomped on some civil rights, but it did work. There was very little sabotage in America throughout the war years, and many Japanese-American lives were saved from citizens looking for revenge from war atrocities committed by the Japanese military. It was no longer possible to imprison large segments of the population, but since the war against the Islamic terrorists and their state sponsors had begun, it was obviously prudent to keep detailed files of that sector of the population.

O'Hallohan started studying the dead men's files he'd just received from Nowiki. When the Secretary called back, Patrick asked if Gustoffson was present and could participate in the call.

"We're in the back of a limo with a partition between us and the driver, and I can put you on the speaker if you believe it's necessary," the Secretary said.

"This better be good," Gustoffson grumbled.

"I think it's imperative." Patrick filled them in on Mike Nowiki's call, highlighting the different titles of the dead terrorists.

"O'Hallohan, you're more of a field agent," the Secretary said. "You're not entrenched in the office. What do you make of this?"

Gustoffson chimed in. "You did well not trusting any one person with this…including me. What do you think?"

"I agree with Nowiki. We've got enemies in country, and they're doing damage. I've read some of the files, especially the dead FBI agent's. There were dozens of security checks on the Arab—sorry, make that Iranian—guy before he was allowed to join the Bureau. He appeared to be as clean as fresh mountain spring water. So how did he get through all our security checks unless he had inside help? And why are the terrorists suddenly bringing him out of deep cover?"

"Do you have any answers to those questions?" the Secretary asked.

"I don't, sir. But I just feel part of the solution is directly in front of me." He got up and started to pace around the office, dragging the phone with him. "All these men were firmly entrenched. What is so important they're willing to give up decades of diligent work?"

"Listen, O'Hallohan. You, Nowiki, and the two of us are the only ones who officially know about these events as possibly being attacks on American soil. Whoever's causing this carnage also knows. Gustoffson and I will select a team and handle the delicate work of sniffing out the moles. You get on this case and figure out why we have terrorists popping out of the ground. Figure out just what the hell is going on out there."

Chapter 19

The Strong Winds

Jesse traced his finger across the blue line representing Interstate 80 in the road atlas. He figured they had about 1,300 miles to travel before getting to San Francisco, another twenty hours of driving, if they didn't break the speed limit. They weren't having much luck with the cops lately.

"If we drive straight through, we can be in San Francisco by this time tomorrow," he said, looking at Leena, who was standing next to the car, the late afternoon sun shining on her face.

"We don't have the final interview scheduled for two more days, Friday afternoon," Leena said.

"I still think we need to drive all night and get as close as possible. We can always stop in Sacramento. It's not very far from San Francisco."

"Good plan, Double-Oh. But can I drive the first stretch until I get tired? Then you can drive through the night while I get my beauty rest." Leena laughed as she spoke, but he noticed that her eyes had lost some of their sparkle.

"I'm surprised you've recovered so quickly from this afternoon's mess," he commented.

"Recovered? Hardly. I cope. When I was just starting out as a young and really dumb reporter, I begged my producer to let me go to Bosnia. I got into a jam there, and the reason I came through okay was because of my cameraman. He was armed. I thought back then if I yelled out, 'Hey I'm a news reporter!' they'd leave us alone." She shook her head. "There was some bloodshed. It was the first time I ever saw someone shot. When I came back, I studied Tae Kwan Do to be able to protect myself. Since then, I've seen a lot of ugliness, truly hell-on-earth butchering. I don't take it to heart anymore."

"A warrior perspective," Jesse said, shaking his head. "I was worried back there that you might have been shot. Hurt. I was so… so very relieved to see you were okay."

"You're so sweet." She reached out, her once polished nails now chipped and dulled, and stroked the back of his hand. "It happened so suddenly that I just started to duck out of the way when the Chinese man—gunman, shooter, agent, whatever—came around the car and started shooting the cop. I don't have any doubt at all that they were real cops. Whoever is behind it, you do realize, they're not going to give up trying to stop us."

"Let them try. They're not up against helpless children."

"Were you this fierce when you were in Vietnam?"

"I was an unworldly, pink-faced teenager that carried a machine gun. Fierce? Maybe. Dangerous? Without a doubt." Jesse grinned. "Maybe more to myself than the enemy, though."

"Why do you say that?"

"I was naïve, like you. It took some time before I understood there are no rules in war. Just survival." He looked at the sun; it was definitely starting to set. "I think it's time to go."

Jesse slid into the back seat and lay down, staring straight up as the darkness overtook them. Deeply buried thoughts kept erupting and then bouncing back and forth like a handball in his mind. He thought about Vietnam all over again. He couldn't change what he had done over there, reliving it for the millionth time. He finally fell into a gray, shifting sleep, the type of sleep that made him feel more tired when he awoke.

Leena woke him with a kiss, running her hand through his hair.

"Where are we?" He tried to distance himself from the dream.

"Just outside of Green River, Wyoming," she said with a tiredness he hadn't previously heard in her voice.

"I feel great!" he lied, sitting up straight. He could tell she saw through him. Busted, he thought.

"This night driving really hurts my eyes," she said instead, allowing him to dance off the hook.

Relieved, the dream running away, he asked, "Is that an age thing?"

"Could be. But I don't mind getting older. It certainly beats the alternative."

"Here, climb in. There's a blanket on the floor covering the M16." Jesse reached down and pulled the blanket to the seat.

"What's in the green bag?"

"Extra ammo, I guess. I forgot about it." He unzipped the bag and placed it on the seat. "There's a LAW in here."

"A what?"

"A rocket launcher, kinda like an RPG. Also extra ammo and two grenades, looks like frags."

"They might come in handy. I hope we don't have to use them," she said and then yawned.

"Me, too. Why don't you crawl in? You're such a tiny thing you'll be able to stretch out and get some good shuteye." He zipped the bag and put it back on the floor.

"Yeah, I know. That's what my dad worried about."

"Getting some sleep?"

"No, stretching out on the back seat."

"Smart man."

"He was. He would have liked you. He liked what he called 'real people.' You fit that description perfectly. Give me a kiss. I'm tired."

He did as she commanded. He hadn't been in love in a long, long time and knew by the ache in his heart that he was well on his way. It occurred to him that he didn't do such a good job of protecting his last and only love and was hoping she would forgive him for loving someone else. He decided to say a silent prayer asking forgiveness, and while he was still connected upstairs he vowed to protect his new almost-lover. With his own life, if need be.

They moved along in what seemed like slow motion for an eternity of hours, until he caught himself drifting off the road for the second time. They were traveling through Salt Lake City, his blinks getting longer, close to being asleep at the wheel. It was 3:30 in the morning, so he took the next exit and found a well-lit, 24-hour Wal-Mart Superstore. He parked the Take-Us in a place that was open and exposed, nothing like camouflage. The more obvious, the better. He stopped the car, locked the doors, and was asleep in mere minutes. No dreams this time.

Jesse could feel the heat on his eyelids. Twice in one week now, he'd come awake with the sun on his face. He didn't want to open his eyes. His head was pounding, and he thought he was getting too old to be sleeping in his car. He cracked one eye partially open and then the other. Leena was still sleeping peacefully.

It took a few seconds for Jesse's internal computer to reboot and figure out where he was. He needed some caffeine. He grabbed the Diet Pepsi from the can holder he'd added to the dash and slammed it. Yuck! Flotistacia.

He soon had the Take-Us in motion and back on the Interstate. He was still in the process of waking up when he felt Leena's hand on his shoulder.

He looked in the rearview mirror "Good morning, sunshine."

"Good morning." She yawned and stretched her arms out. "Why are we going south toward Provo?"

"What do you mean?"

"The road sign up ahead." She pointed. "That's the exit for Provo. Did I miss something? Why are we on I-15 South?"

"Oh, shit, I must have made a wrong turn last night."

"Shhh, shhh." She rubbed his shoulder. "Don't be so crabby. Where's the map?" Jesse handed it back across the seat to her. She studied it for a moment.

"We can get off at the next exit and flip a U-turn. No, wait, if we go up here maybe twenty miles, we can get on Highway 6 and that takes us to Highway 50. It's actually a shorter and faster way to go than I-80."

"I've traveled Highway 50 before. It's a pretty deserted stretch of road."

"True. Nevertheless, we know they're searching for us. Don't you think it more likely they would be watching the Interstate? We might be able to sneak by them."

While she finished speaking, Jesse stared into passing car windows. Looking for what? An enemy's face? A gun? "All right, what can it hurt?"

He continued to drive south, eventually getting on Highway 50 at Delta, Utah. Soon after, they pulled into a truck stop that advertised a large breakfast, cheap.

"Bet you could go for one of those fat-soaked, cholesterol-laden, heart-busting breakfast bombs they're offering, couldn't you?" Leena asked, getting out of the car.

Jesse was far beyond stiff now. "Maybe two. When was the last time I ate?"

"Seems like a year ago. Come on, I've got to tinkle." She started walking quickly to the door. They ordered breakfast and then took turns going to the restroom, where they each did a little personal grooming. The waitress brought the food before Leena returned. Jesse was deep into his eggs when Leena came back and stood over the table. Her smile had disappeared and her eyes had a faraway look.

"What's wrong?" he asked.

"I checked my voice mail. It's my mom. Listen to her message." Leena pushed a button on her phone.

He put the phone to his ear. "Sweetie, you are so kind. The painters showed up this morning. They told me you contracted to have the house repainted. The older man said it was a surprise present from you. The three of them, all Mexicans, started doing the prep work. That's what they call it. He gave me some samples and said I can pick any color I want. I'm kinda tired of this green, and I think a warm cream color would be nice, maybe with two different colors of trim. That does seem to be the style. Call me when you have time. You are so sweet. I love you."

"So?"

"I didn't contract to have her house painted."

"Let me hear that again." He listened a second time. "She said

Mexicans, but it could be Middle-Eastern men," he said and then added, "She said three."

"Is that significant?"

"There were three in both the troopers' car and the Toyota. Could that be how they structure their…teams? Units?"

"Cells. Three-man cells."

"Cells, yeah."

"Islamic terrorists at my mom's house."

"So they're watching your mom. They could be using her for bait."

"God, this is terrible." She sat down abruptly. "What do we do?"

He looked sorrowfully at his breakfast, picked up two pieces of bacon, held them up, and made a cross with them as if he was trying to ward off evil spirits. "You know Muslims believe if they touch or eat pork, they won't be allowed into Paradise. I think I'll coat some bullets with these pieces of bacon." He picked up his coffee cup and drained it. "Let's go, we'll figure something out on the way." He threw a twenty on the table, grasped Leena's hand and they walked out.

It was time for the Take-Us to take off. The road was deserted and he continuously increased his speed. It wasn't long before they were clipping along at a hundred miles an hour in the flat sections between the mountain passes. They passed a sign that proclaimed the road to be the loneliest highway in America.

They'd been driving for about three and a half hours when Jesse saw a dot on the horizon. It got steadily closer and he finally identified it as a helicopter. He slowed down, which was a good thing because it was a sheriff's chopper. It passed over them low and slow, giving them a good look. Then it made a one-eighty behind them and flew back over them in the same direction it had come from. It wasn't long before it disappeared from sight.

"What did you think of that?" Leena asked.

"Seemed innocent enough."

"It sure is easy to get paranoid. They can't all be bad, can they?"

"I don't see how. Is that a gas station up ahead? I gotta go…bad."

"Good idea. I'm thirsty for something besides this." Leena held up a bottle of water.

"Don't we have another Monster Energy drink back there somewhere?"

"I think you drank it yesterday."

"I did? Jeez, time zooms past when you're on holiday."

"Maybe we should shoot today's update while we're there," she said looking out through the windshield.

"Good idea. No one will be able to figure out where we are from this backdrop. Everything looks the same. Pucker bushes and scrub, all desert."

They turned into the dirt parking lot of a faded little store with two gas pumps and passed an elderly couple in a blue Ford station wagon that was pulling out. They returned their waves as the couple left. Jesse parked next to the gas pumps and began washing the dead bugs from the windshield. Leena went inside the store. When he had finished, Jesse followed the signs to the restrooms located on the side of the building. He came out and looked around. Except for this building and a pink trailer next to it, there wasn't much to see. There were no other structures in sight. It was totally isolated. He walked back around the corner and went inside. It was a small, dusty place: half store and half bar. Leena was having an earnest conversation with an old man who was wearing a cowboy hat and standing behind the bar.

"Jesse, this is Walt. He owns the place."

"Glad to meet you, Walt. Great place you got here. Like an oasis in the desert." Jesse put his hand out and shook with the old cowboy. He looked as dried up as the desert outside, with the exception of his eyes. They sparkled like the cold, refreshing water of a deep mountain pool.

"Thanks. It's a pleasure to meet ya, young feller. I was just tellin' the pretty lady here I'd like to git my hands on one of them cars you got. I saw it on TV. Out here we only got power from the generator. Be a lot cheaper if I had that car."

"It might be a while before they're on the market. So you'll have to make do with what you have, for now," Jesse said, putting both hands up.

"Figured that, sonny. Just sayin' you need to get this new car out to common folk—"

"Listen, Jesse," Leena said, interrupting. "Walt was just telling me the sheriff in the helicopter stopped by not long ago."

"Yep, dropped right outta the sky. He was lookin' for an old Buick like yours, only it was yeller. Told him I ain't seen nothin' yeller all day."

"Is the sheriff a big Indian guy?" Jesse asked.

"He ain't so big, more like a little runt. But yeah, he's dark like an Injun. So were his two cronies."

"Hey, Walt, I appreciate you being nice to my lady friend." Jesse winked at Leena. "When this car starts getting mass produced, I'll make sure you get one of the first ones."

"Lookie here, Jesse, I ain't done nothin' to deserve that."

"You've been very kind, and that deserves a nice gesture in return," Leena said, giving him one of her special TV smiles.

"Maybe so, but nobody does that no more," the old cowboy said with a shake of his head.

They said their goodbyes and headed to the car.

"Maybe I'm not so paranoid after all," Leena said. "I'll get the camera from the trunk. We'll just have to do the interview on the way."

While Leena was getting the camera, Jesse got the map out. "I can't find another highway we can take and get off this road," he said as he handed her the road atlas.

She studied the book. "Nothing for at least fifty, maybe seventy miles."

"We have to figure they'll try some kind of ambush."

"I couldn't agree more," she said.

He stared directly into her blue eyes. "Listen, maybe—"

Leena turned her back and stomped away.

"No, you are not going to dump me here. They have my mom!" she yelled, opening the door to the Take-Us and reaching behind to uncover the M16 and LAW rocket. She put the LAW on her lap. "How do you work this thing? And what the hell does LAW mean?"

"Light anti-tank weapon," Jesse answered, thinking he'd go up against a whole company of tanks with her by his side.

About twenty miles from Walt's place, the road turned downhill, coming off another mountain pass. The visibility was great even though the wind was blowing like crazy, creating dust devils in the distance. Jesse could make out a car parked just off to the side of the highway a couple miles ahead.

When they got closer, he saw it was the blue Ford station wagon they'd seen pulling out of the store earlier. There was no one around the car that he could see from this distance. When they were about a half mile from the car, he could see dust spiraling upward from a small swale about a quarter of a mile away and parallel to the Ford. The dust looked like rotor wash from a helicopter, just like he'd seen in Vietnam.

He knew.

"Hold on!" he yelled, at the same time pushing his right foot all the way down.

They'd been traveling at about eighty miles per hour, and the Take-Us leapt forward. Jesse's hands were sweating when he took a quick glance down. The speedometer was pegged at 200 when they came abreast of the little blue Ford. He could see two bodies slumped over in the front seat.

Then KAWHOMP! The station wagon disintegrated into smoke and flames, a deadly spray of parts and shrapnel flying indiscriminately in all directions.

He saw it all in his rearview mirror. The Take-Us was already past. The terrorists were too slow on the trigger, accustomed to slow-traveling Humvees when they set off their IEDs.

"Wow, that looked just like the pictures we get from Iraq," Leena said, turning and looking through the back window. "Oh shit! Here they come!"

"You're starting to talk like me," he said in a forced, cool voice, concentrating fully on his driving.

"Yeah. Great. What are we going to do now?"

"The Take-Us is faster than the helicopter. They're flying into a headwind. We have a small window of time to find a place where we can choose the battleground. See those mountains ahead? They'll catch us there."

Time seemed to stand still.

"You're right. They're falling farther behind."

The helicopter was a small dot on the horizon when they slowed for the twisting ascent up the mountain pass. As they negotiated a hairpin curve, they slowed further and the helicopter was getting much larger.

"They're really closing the gap," Leena said, her voice steady, one hand on the armrest, the other on the dash, trying to brace herself.

"Okay!" Jesse turned the steering wheel abruptly to the left around another tight curve, all four tires screeching in protest.

They lost sight of the helicopter in some trees around a tight bend in the road.

"Where are they? Where…There! They'll be on us in just a few minutes." Leena pointed, her voice indicating no fear, just fact. She had already gathered the weapons and placed them in the front seat.

The Take-Us was close to the top of the mountain. Around the next tight corner—there it was—he'd found the killing field.

"Here's where we'll make our stand," he shouted, adrenaline pounding though his veins.

There was plenty of room to pull the car off the road. About forty feet from the car was a large jumble of rocks to hide behind. The mountain was to their back. There was only one way to approach them from the air. He jabbed on the brakes and brought the car to an abrupt halt in dust as thick as snow. Jesse seized the rifle, and Leena handed him the LAW rocket.

Leena took the pistol and started to run for the rock cover, but suddenly stopped and turned. She ran back to the car, reached in, and grabbed the camera. She had almost made it back to the rocks when the helicopter came screaming overhead.

The pilot saw the car, banked immediately to his left, and flew in an easy circle to slow down. Only then did he start to approach, slowly repositioning the helicopter so the right side was toward Jesse and Leena. The reason was soon obvious: the side door was open and there were two men—one sitting in the rear seat and the other lying on the floor—holding what looked like AK-47 assault rifles.

One of the men pointed to where Leena had dashed into the rocks. She had crawled and squirmed her way deeper to her left and had the camera aimed at the helicopter. The two men began shooting into the rocks, dust rising and rock chips flying everywhere. The noise was incredibly loud with the whop-whop-whop of the helicopter blades and the deep stutter of the rifles.

One thing Jesse had learned about helicopters was that when they were moving and bouncing around, they were terrible gun-firing platforms. It was very difficult to shoot accurately from a chopper. Add in the high winds shaking the aluminum bird and he figured the shooters couldn't hit the car, let alone two people hidden among the rocks.

The pilot had his hands full trying as best he could to keep the helicopter stable. One of the men in back could see their fire was not effective. He gestured to the pilot, who realized his mistake and started to edge the machine closer. There wasn't enough room to land on the road because of the guardrails that protected vehicles from running off the sheer cliff directly below the helicopter.

Jesse hadn't hidden in the same clump of rocks that Leena chose. Instead, he'd run farther up the road and was almost directly in front of the pilot. He telescoped the weapon to ready and had the pop-up sight aimed at the center of the pilot's chest.

"Come a little bit closer to the road," Jesse said softly to himself. "Come on, just a little bit more."

He hadn't fired a LAW since Vietnam, over thirty-five years before. BRASS: that was the acronym the Army taught. Breathe, Relax, Aim…S…what was the S for? Fuck it. He squeezed the trigger.

Whoosh! The rocket shot out straight and hot. The pilot glanced at the dazzling rocket blast, but he was too late to react. The rocket went though his Plexiglas windshield and pierced his chest. There was a bright flash and huge explosion. The main rotor snapped off and went Frisbee-ing though the air. The helicopter hung for a split second, then flipped onto its side and disappeared from view as it plunged down the sheer cliff. Only the smoke and stench remained.

Jesse ran to the other side of the road, clutching the M16 and scanning downward. He couldn't see much of anything below a large outcropping of rocks, just smoke trailing from far below.

Leena came up behind him.

"You okay, sweetheart?" he asked, relief evident in his voice.

"Yeah, perfectly—they were lousy shots. What's with the 'sweetheart'? That's twice today."

He put his arms around her and kissed her gently.

"You're shaking," she said.

"After-action jitters."

"You know, you're kind of good to have around in a pinch."

He squeezed her so close to him all she could do was stand there, her arms pinned to her sides, with the camera in one hand and the pistol in the other.

"I got it all," Leena said when Jesse finally broke the embrace. "Maybe I'll win an Emmy."

"We'd better go," he said, still unnerved and still worried. "There might be more on the way, and you don't want to be awarded that Emmy posthumously."

They scrambled into the car and started driving down the mountain once again.

"I don't think any others are on the way," Leena said. "We're too far out in the desert. They would have to have some kind of special communication device to reach someone way out here. My sat phone won't work in a helicopter. I tried it before in New York. And I don't think they'd dare speak over a regular radio."

"That's a good take, Double-Oh Seven-and-a-half."

"No, really, they wouldn't be brazen enough to come that far out into the open."

"They've been pretty bold so far."

"Not really. Think about their ambush sites."

"Okay. Let's say you're correct. What's next?" Jesse started to slow his speed. He was going over a hundred and twenty…probably matching his heartbeat.

"I think we're going to have to figure out a plan to get my mom out. And—"

"I've got an idea. We'll be in Carson City in three hours, maybe a little more. We're going to need some dark clothes and a few other goodies."

"What kind of an idea? No, wait a minute. While I'm thinking about it— God, I hate to bring it up—but we need to get today's' update done and sent out. It's after three o'clock on the East Coast."

"Do you think we should continue, considering what's been happening to us?" He looked at her skeptically.

"Absolutely. If we don't, they're already starting to win. It's not about us any longer. It's so much bigger now. If they kill this story they'll eventually crush the life out of us all."

"Do we have to stop, or can you film inside the car?" he asked, convinced.

"I think if I get in the back seat and you turn to face me a few times…Yeah, that should do it…I'll be able to pan outside once in a while when you're speaking. If it doesn't work, we'll just have to stop and set up outside somewhere."

"Okay, let's do it."

"I would love to, but we better do the filming instead."

Jesse laughed, feeling his tension drain away. "You are just impossible."

***

"This is Leena Delaney, once again 'On the Road' with the surprising Take-Us automobile. This time I'm filming from inside the auto as we travel through the desert."

Filming really isn't the correct term since there is no longer any film used, Jesse thought as she spoke. The correct term would be digitizing. "Yes," he said in response to her lead-in. "One of the pleasant surprises of this car is the excellent stability and control it has. I removed the original engine and transmission, replacing them with batteries. I located the batteries very low in the frame, and because of the extreme weight and the location, along with the wide wheelbase and width of these older cars, this auto positively hugs the road. I suppose many of you are concerned that the Take-Us car is a…well, a turtle. That couldn't be further from the truth. I've taken this car up to 200 miles per hour. That was on a special test section of road, I might add. Because the motors are direct drive and there are no friction-robbing gears or transmission, it's very fast in the quarter mile. The Take-Us probably isn't as fast as some of the production automobiles being manufactured today, mostly because of its size and weight. However, the other side of that coin is that the car is very safe. It's as comfortable to ride in as any car currently being manufactured as a luxury model, but much quieter. And of course, it uses no gasoline."

"Accelerate again, Jesse, so we can show the speed." Leena focused on the speedometer as Jesse quickly took it up past 120 miles per hour.

Leena switched off the camera. "That will piss off a bunch of people," she said with soft malice in her voice, an entirely different voice than the one she used on stage. She put the camera in the back window and hit the transmit button.

"While I'm back here, I think I'll take a short nap. It might be a long night." Leena placed a small kiss on the back of Jesse's neck. "Wake me when we get to Carson City, sweetheart. Sweetheart…I like the sound of that."

Day Four

Chapter 20

The Innocent Eyes

Sheriff Chuck Trojanowski was starting to wear down and had decided to go home early that night. He was at home now, sitting in his favorite chair and reading the paper. The TV was on and the news reporters were blathering in the background. Two days had flown by since the discovery of his deputy, the traitor. The whole thing was a train wreck. The incident had taken place just down the road from his home. The FBI had given him a heads-up when they examined the laptop computer. Much had been deleted and not yet restored, but there wasn't any doubt that his deputy had been receiving email and communicating online with his handler, who was presumably in the Middle East. So far, thank God, the press had not gotten hold of the story.

The department, along with the agents from DHS and FBI, were currently going through reports in his office, trying to find any damage the deputy spy might have caused. It was going to be a long process. Trojanowski increased the number of Rolaids he normally took for his stomach as he thought about the inevitable political fallout when it finally became clear that he was the one who ultimately hired the traitor.

"Daddy, there's the man that was in my barn."

"Mmmm…okay, Joey."

"He's in the desert now."

"Who?"

"That man right there," Joey said, pointing at the TV screen.

The sheriff lowered his paper and looked at the man talking

about some kind of car that he was obviously driving. "What do you mean 'in your barn'?"

"The barn where me and Bobby play. The one with all that yellow tape around it now."

"The one just down road?"

Joey nodded several times. "Yeah, that's the one."

"How do you know that man on the TV was in there?"

"I saw him. He was in my barn on TV."

"When?"

"Right here."

"I mean what day?"

"He's here every day on TV."

Sheriff Trojanowski watched the remainder of the report, then got up and went to his study. It was no use trying to quiz his five-year-old anymore. He opened his briefcase to pull out his list of contact phone numbers and punched in the number he had for Agent Nowiki. The agent was out in the field, but after a few inquires the local office gave him the phone number for Homeland Security. He passed through the automated phone answering system until finally he heard a live voice.

"This is Night Duty Officer Patrick O'Hallohan. How may I be of assistance?" O'Hallohan's shift had started a little over an hour ago, but he'd been there all day, stopping only for a couple of hours to catch a few z's.

"This is Sheriff Chuck Trojanowski from St. Joseph County, Indiana. I spoke to Agent Nowiki's office at the FBI, and they gave me this number."

"Yes, sir, I recognize your name. I've been studying the reports for the last two days. It's turning into a genuine mystery."

"Maybe I can help you a bit with that. Tonight my five-year-old son identified the person who was in the barn."

"The barn your deputy was found in?"

"Yes."

"He actually saw someone in the barn?" O'Hallohan sat up straight to be ready to write on the notepad in front of him.

"Well, kind of. Have you been paying attention to a series of reports that WCN has been airing for the last few days about a new type of car? They call it the Take-Us automobile."

"No, all I've seen is the nonstop reporting on Senator Charlton. I turned it off before I puked."

"Yeah, I know. Well Joey, my five-year-old son, said he recognized the inside of the barn on TV. It must have been broadcast earlier in the week."

"No shit! I haven't seen any of those TV reports. I think we can pull them up. Hold on." O'Hallohan put the sheriff on hold and motioned to one of his assistants, explaining what he wanted. They found the videos in a couple of minutes.

"Okay, Sheriff, I have the video on a monitor in front of me. Can I download some of these pictures of the barn for you to identify? You have email where you're at now?"

"Sure, send them now and you can put me on hold until I look at them." He gave O'Hallohan his email address. In just a few minutes, the photos started coming through. He looked at them and then called for Joey. "Is this the picture you saw of the barn?"

"Sure, Daddy. See the old signs on the walls?"

After he'd put the sheriff on hold, Patrick watched the entire segment. "Sheriff, you still there?" he asked through the speakerphone.

"Sure. Me and my boy can for sure say the barn in the picture is the same place my...man...was found."

"Thanks, Sheriff. I hope this is going to open this whole thing up."

"It's the least I can do. My man started this, right?" He still could not bring himself to say deputy.

Patrick was prepared to say he couldn't tell the sheriff anything, and then thought, this is a real lawman, not a talking head. "Sheriff, this is really ugly and super-secret, but you should know that you aren't the only one who's been deceived by these bastards."

"Thanks. And I mean it from the bottom of my heart." Trojanowski blew out a sigh of relief. "Your secret is safe with me."

After he ended the call, Patrick started to review all the interviews from WCN on the Take-Us car. He began to appreciate the depth of the impact this car was going to have on the world. He dug out a road map and had started to study it when he was interrupted with another incoming call on his private line.

"O'Hallohan. This is Mike Nowiki, FBI."

"Let me guess. More dead terrorists?"

"Three. You starting to get clairvoyant, or what?"

"No, I'm starting to get a handle on what's going on. Where are you?"

"In a jet. Somewhere over Wyoming or Utah. We're on our way to Nevada."

"Where in Nevada?" O'Hallohan looked down at the map in front of him. "Wait, let me guess. Someplace off Interstate 80."

"Wrong, Highway 50. Way out in the middle of nowhere."

O'Hallohan deflated a little. "Okay, what happened this time?"

"Helicopter crash. Belonged to the local sheriff's department. They believe one of the bodies belonged to the pilot, a deputy sheriff of Middle-Eastern descent."

"What do you mean they 'believe' it was the pilot?"

"They could only find the bottom half of his body, but he's the only deputy unaccounted for. And that's not the kicker. They also found a laptop computer and two AK-47s alongside the other two male bodies. Both men were—what the hell—Arabs. The two automatic rifles had recently been fired."

"I think I know who the target was. How did the helicopter crash?"

"Don't know yet. One of the officers at the scene, former military, said it looked like it was shot down. I'll know more when I get to the crash site…But wait! Did you say you know who they were shooting at?"

"I've just received a tip. I'm working on it right now. Give me a call in a few hours with an update, and I'll share my hypothesis with you."

After hanging up, Patrick watched all the videos from WCN one more time. He started to run a time line. The girl was very clever. She never gave away their exact location. She must have known from the onset they were going to be pursued. That was an interesting thought. He wondered what information DHS might have on her and jotted himself a note. He compared their route to the three events that had happened. Even though he didn't know exactly where in Nevada the last one occurred, they easily could have been in each location.

So he now had the *why* and the *where*. How about the *who*? He didn't know anything about Jesse Christenson, the inventor of the car. He set the massive computers to work gathering that information. While he was waiting, he decided to give WCN a call and see what they could tell him.

WCN eventually routed him to Kellie, Miss Delaney's personal assistant—a modern way of saying secretary. "Miss Delaney's office, how can I help ya?" She was peeved she had to work overtime.

"This is Agent Patrick O'Hallohan from Homeland Security. I'm calling on an urgent matter of national security. I just viewed all Ms. Delaney's reports on the Take-Us car and was wondering if there's any additional footage that hasn't been put on the air."

"There's always additional footage," Kellie said in a snotty Bronx accent. "Bleeps and such."

"I'm sorry to bother you, but I meant anything out of the ordinary," he said, wondering what crawled up her skirt.

"It's funny you should ask. Somehow a helicopter got imposed on today's update. We didn't think much of it because she didn't say anything about it. It was like she was practicing with the camera while watchin' a movie or somethin', ya know? Would ya like to see it?"

"Please. Could you send it to my email?"

After she agreed, he gave her the address, hung up, and busied himself until he checked and saw that she had sent the video. He opened the attachment and, indeed, there was a helicopter. It looked like an OH-58 Kiowa, approaching from the side. Two men were firing their automatic rifles, which could have been AK-47s, at the camera. One of the men gestured to the pilot and the helicopter starting moving closer to the camera. The sound was on and he could hear the noise of the rotor blades and the harsh snap of the guns. Suddenly there was a blazing flash and a deafening explosion. The helicopter disappeared from sight. He then heard a female's voice saying, "Drop dead, motherfuckers."

Before the camera was turned off, he saw the Take-Us car in the foreground, only now it was black.

"Sir," he said into the phone after dialing the direct line. "I've got it." He had just finished reading the information the computer had developed.

"Who is this? Got what?" Gustoffson asked.

"Sorry. Patrick O'Hallohan, sir. The answer to the Threat Level Red condition—I mean, I know what's triggering all the terrorist chatter and activity."

"Go on."

"It's the Take-Us car."

"Take-Us car? Where did I see—?"

"WCN," Patrick interrupted. He went on, explaining his entire theory.

"Good work. We'll send out a message to law enforcement to bring them in."

After a moment's hesitation, O'Hallohan said, "Sir, I don't think that would be a prudent course of action. What with the infiltration of the enemy into our law enforcement agencies—including federal, state, and police departments across the nation—it just might get Christenson and the female reporter killed. And if I were in their situation, I wouldn't trust any cop. That's probably why they haven't sought any help."

This time it was Gustoffson's turn to hesitate. "Yeah, I see what you mean. We'll get a team of our own together, people we know we can trust."

"Sir…uh…"

"What now?"

"Well, if I were them, I'd think twice and maybe shoot first if the person who approached me looked Middle Eastern."

"That's also a good point." There was a note of respect in his voice. "What do you recommend?"

"I would like to go. Sir. In case you haven't noticed, I'm of Irish ancestry. With my red hair and blue eyes it would be hard to confuse me with the enemy."

"All right, get to Andrews Air Force Base. There will be a car waiting for you out front and a jet at the base. Wait a minute, where are you going to go?"

"The same place they're going. Home."

Chapter 21

The Hometown Hero

Jesse bid adios to Highway 50 outside of Carson City and after ten miles turned onto Highway 88. They crossed into California a short time later and traveled westbound through Hope Valley—in his opinion, one of the prettiest places in the entire United States. Tonight there was only a sliver of moon, and the darkness hid the wild but tranquil beauty of the place. The Take-Us easily climbed the steep, winding mountain road of the Sierra Nevada and rolled through Kit Carson Pass at more than 8,000 feet above sea level. A half hour later he turned off the main highway, drove a short block, and pulled into the tree-lined access road that led to his church's parking lot. They parked in the furthermost rear corner, hiding the car from any road traffic by a thicket of trees.

Jesse was almost home.

The cool night air was normal for this time of year in the Sierras. Jesse and Leena dressed outside, next to the car. Each had bought black, long-sleeved Under Armour, athletic shirts, and skintight, black, bicycle-riding pants.

"Are you looking at my butt again?" Leena asked.

"Uh, yeah. I am."

"Good. I was beginning to think you'd forgotten about me."

"Never, ever." He put on some black socks and, using the black spray paint they had left over from painting the car, sprayed his white Nikes. He handed the can of paint to Leena.

"Do you think this is really necessary?" she asked, a little miffed.

"Only if you don't want to be seen."

"I just bought these shoes before we left New York City."

"Come on, get off your wallet," he said, once again putting his foot in his mouth. "I'll buy you a new pair tomorrow."

"You are a stupid, stupid man," Leena said, grabbing for the can of paint. "Cute, but stupid." She smiled, then, and slipped into his arms, giving him a passionate kiss. "Just don't do anything stupid tonight."

"Look, maybe we should call for some help," he said, a little doubt starting to well up. "We could—"

"We've already talked about this. Who can we trust to show up? They have millions of dollars and can buy anybody. One call and my mom dies." She bent down and started spray-painting her shoes.

"You're right," he said after she straightened back up. "Here's your hat and your night-vision goggles." The black ski mask had holes cut out for her eyes. "Have you ever used night-vision before?"

"No, but the owner of the store in Carson City showed me how they work."

"They're kind of freaky, at first. Everything looks ghostly, but you'll soon get the hang of it." She had her dark gloves on when he handed her the pistol. "Did you remember your mom's house key?"

"Got it right here," she said, putting the pistol over her left breast.

"I wish these straps were more heavy duty. This model of goggles is probably the sit-in-your-car and spy-on-your-cheating-husband variety."

"I'm just thankful we could find these." She slipped the goggles on as they started walking out of the parking lot.

The air had a sweet scent to it. A night smell.

Holding hands, they began the walk to Malie's house, almost a mile away. They stayed mostly to the edge of the road. On occasion, they could hear the small sound of gravel crunching beneath their feet. There was no traffic this late at night, which was normal for this sleepy little community. But even so, they were prepared to dive behind a tree or bush at the slightest sound.

Jesse had walked this route many times from his house to the store, which was just a block farther than the church. There was also a shortcut though the forest and around the big hill they were walking down.

Leena was in front of Jesse, and he took off the goggles, looking directly at her. It would be hard for someone to see her. The black of her clothing blended perfectly with the blackness of the night. When they arrived at the bottom of the hill, he shifted the M16 and put the night-vision goggles back on. They turned off the road, cut across a field, and entered the small woods that ended at the back of Malie's property. Neither of them had spoken since they'd left the parking lot. Jesse placed his hand on Leena's shoulder and she stopped.

He now knew they were watching her house. He could see the outline of someone sitting next to her mother's garage. The man was cradling some kind of weapon and appeared to be asleep.

Jesse gave Leena's shoulder a squeeze. She nodded in silent assent and hid behind a tree. He retreated slowly and walked quietly through a long field of tall grasses and weeds until reaching the seasonal creek bed that ran along his property line one hundred feet from his house. He crept up the dry watercourse until he was parallel to the back corner of the house.

Last fall, after he'd started converting the Take-Us car, he'd also started planning for what Leena called his just-in-case scenario. He installed French drains with the pretext of draining the surface water that comes from the heavy rains in the winter. It was easy to sneak a man-made tunnel in at the same time.

The entrance to the twenty-four-inch tunnel was easily visible with the goggles. He took off the fencing that kept the tunnel from becoming a home to the many skunks that frequented the neighborhood. Then he put the M16 inside the tunnel, got in, and began crawling toward the house. He reached the end, which was under the house, without any trouble. He climbed the short ladder built for just such occasions, though he'd thought it would be used for escape, not to gain entry. There was a cleverly disguised hole cut through the plywood in the floor of the walk-in closet in his bedroom. He pushed up to open it and peek out. Everything appeared to be in its place. The loaded sixteen-gauge shotgun his dad had given him on his sixteenth birthday still stood in the corner, undisturbed. He climbed out of the crawl space and took hold of the shotgun.

Feeling the thick carpet beneath his feet, he cautiously headed out of the room and started down the hallway. The plan was to go out onto the back deck, which was just off the living room. Once there, he would fire a couple of shots into the air, turn on some lights, and get the flying fuck out of there. His logic was that if the terrorists were watching Malie's house, they'd be drawn to him like a fly to shit.

God, he prayed silently, let this work.

Something didn't feel right, and the hair on the back of his neck stood at attention as he started to step down into the living room.

Jesse saw him right away.

The son of a bitch was sitting in his chair looking out his window.

The floor betrayed Jesse at that precise moment, letting out a tiny creak.

Startled, the man stood up and turned in Jesse's direction.

"Freeze! Don't move!" Jesse yelled. It always seemed to work in the movies.

The man said something foreign with the word "fuck" in the middle and started to raise the automatic weapon in his right hand.

Jesse didn't hesitate. He pulled the trigger on his forty-year-old pump shotgun from its position next to his hip. The *click* was amazingly loud in the solid darkness. Oh, shit! He'd forgotten to pump a shell into the chamber.

There was a bright muzzle flash, made even brighter by the night vision goggles, as the intruder began shooting.

Jesse felt a hot, poking burn in his left side as he fell to the floor and began to pump in a shell at the same time.

The sound of gunfire in his ears was deafening.

The man didn't have night vision and was spraying bullets blindly at the place where Jesse had just been standing. Rolling once, Jesse took aim and fired, blowing the man off his feet and halfway through the elegant Andersen windows. He pumped another shell in and fired again, this time knocking the intruder the rest of the way through the window and onto the sidewalk outside.

A terrorist in the front yard opened fire.

Bullets began crashing into the living room wall and fireplace, knocking pictures off the wall and breaking the hurricane lamps, which were full of oil.

Jesse felt for the hole in his side. It was leaking blood. He pumped another shell into the shotgun, despite the fact that his bloody hand kept slipping off the shotgun. He crawled forward, raised the shotgun, and pointed it through the broken window. Without aiming, he let off another blast.

Headlights came on across the street, and a vehicle came barreling down his neighbor's driveway, almost directly across from his driveway. It slammed to a stop about thirty feet from the house.

Jesse raised his head and sneaked a peek.

It was a sheriff's SUV.

He ducked back down just as he saw the white-hot muzzle blast from a shotgun. Oh shit, not again. Broken glass showered down on him, and the oil from the broken lamps caught fire.

Jesse poked the shotgun out the broken front window and blindly fired one more time.

Another set of headlights turned into the driveway. There were so many gunshots going off it sounded like Vietnam. Good God, what had he gotten himself into? This was worse than some of the most furious firefights he'd been in. If he didn't move soon, this would be the end of it all. He began crawling toward the foyer as fast as possible, the glass from his beautiful windows cutting his free hand and knees. A blast from an automatic weapon tore through the front door and chipped the tiles directly in front of his face.

Jesse pointed the shotgun at the front door, expecting the worst, and tried to remember how many shots he'd fired. Damn, might be empty, he thought. "Gotta go, gotta go," he said aloud and jumped up as bullets continued to ping around.

He sprinted down the hallway, finally getting back to the walk-in closet. He dropped into the escape hatch and closed the trap door. As he crawled toward the end of the tunnel, his breath came in gasps. Leaving his trusty old shotgun, he grabbed the M16 rifle, willed some strength back into his body, and slowly emerged from the tunnel. That's when he wondered if there might be a welcoming committee at this end of his man-made tunnel.

There was only the night to greet him. He turned and jogged back down the creek bed, his body running on adrenaline, his wounds hardly noticeable. He didn't worry about the noise. It still sounded like a target range out front. Every dog in the neighborhood was barking.

Jesse reached the end of the creek bed, turned right, and started climbing the steep hill. There was very dense undergrowth, mostly mountain misery and manzanita mixed with tall sugar pines, at the bottom of the hill.

It had been a few years since he had been on this deer trail, and even with the night vision goggles it was difficult to make out. He slogged his way up the hill and stopped to lean against a tall pine tree near the top to catch his breath. The wound in his side was beginning to shout for attention.

He glanced back and saw flames licking the roof of his house. The bastards! Before his mind could get heavy with his anger, he caught sight of a figure seventy-five yards below.

Behind Jesse, the moon was in its last quarter.

Holy shit! He was silhouetted. He stepped behind the tree with barely a second to spare. The bark flew off the tree, and he heard the report of an automatic rifle.

He dropped down as another burst slammed around him. A limb caught his night-vision goggles and ripped them from his head. He grunted aloud at the pain in his side when he hit the ground. He was suddenly blind, lying prone on the ground. He thrashed around in the darkness but couldn't find the goggles.

Dammit! Now what? The path took a steep turn just ahead. "Gotta go, gotta go!" he yelled. As he rose up, he ripped off a burst of gunfire in his adversary's general direction. Then, in a low crouch, he ran up the path around the corner. Once again he heard firing behind him, this time a lot of it, but he was temporarily safe with the hill between him and the shooter.

Jesse started to run, then stopped in his tracks. If he continued back to the church, he'd lead them right to Leena. His ragged breathing was strained and heavy. He could try to cut and run…try to lead them away. No, enough running. It was time to end this. Right now.

He scanned the terrain and saw a downed pine tree twenty feet away on the uphill side of the path. It would have to do. A couple of quick steps and he was off the trail. He jumped over, then crouched behind,, the downed tree and took out the grenades stuffed in the pocket of his shirt, laying them on the tree. The selector switch on his rifle was set to full automatic.

It would be enough.

This was exactly like the ambushes they'd set in Vietnam. It seemed to take forever for the enemy to walk into your trap. It was strange, but if he'd never set foot in Nam, he wouldn't now be capable of firing the LAW, or be able to sit calmly waiting to blow away one of his fellow human beings, enemy or not. He remembered back to Nam when he'd been in this same predicament. Even then he'd wondered if the German soldiers in World War II or the American volunteers in the Revolutionary War—or even the Romans way back when—had felt the same excitement mixed with fear while they waited to spring their traps.

The last time he'd done this, there was a woman.

It was after dark, and his squad had set up an ambush on a trail with a horseshoe bend. When the enemy filled the kill zone, the claymores and grenades roared. In the flashing light, he saw an enemy soldier directly in front of him. He poured his fire into the gook. When the ambush was over and all was still, they went forward to check them out. She was carrying an AK-47 assault rifle in one arm and a small child in the other. He had killed them both in the darkness. It wasn't long after that he'd been wounded and sent home on a stretcher. The wounds in his leg hurt, but the worse wound was inside his head.

It had never healed.

Now in front of him he saw a light bobbing up and down on the trail and heard the soft crunch of leaves. A man had just come around the bend, using a small flashlight trained on the trail. This was going to be easy. He tightened his finger on the trigger. He could see well enough in the weak moonlight to make out that the man had a rifle slung over his shoulder.

BRASS. The words came silently to his lips: breathe, relax, aim, squeeze.

"Stop! Don't move!" The sound of his own voice surprised Jesse. It flashed through his mind that maybe he wasn't the same man he'd been in the jungle thirty-seven years before. "I have an M16 targeted on you."

The man stopped dead in his tracks. "This is a good spot for an ambush. I would have chosen it myself," the man said, a tone of admiration in his voice.

"You need to slip that rifle off your shoulder and let it fall to the ground, easy-like."

Leaves crunched as the rifle landed next to the trail. "Mr. Christenson, I'm a federal agent—"

"Sure, I've heard that one before."

"Yeah, I bet you have."

"If that's true, then why were you shooting at me?"

"I wasn't shooting at you. I shot the terrorist that was shooting at you. You were being followed."

"What?" Jesse wondered if, in all the excitement, there could have been two different guns firing.

"I'll prove it. Just let me shine this light into my face," the man said and started to move the light up.

"Stop!" Jesse shouted. The man froze. "Okay, take it slow. But if you shine that light in my direction, I'll cut you in half."

The man carefully pointed the light up into his face. Jesse could see red hair and blue eyes looking back at him. "Okay, I get it. You don't look like an Arab. They could have bought you."

"Yeah, they could have, but would I have come around this bend with my rifle over my shoulder? I knew you'd be waiting somewhere up ahead. It's what I would have done."

"Who are you?"

"Agent Patrick O'Hallohan, Homeland Security. I know about the confrontations you had in the barn in Indiana and on the road in Nebraska. I even know about the helicopter you shot down in Nevada. What did you use? An RPG?"

"LAW rocket."

"Where did you find one of those? They're antiques."

"So am I. Long story," Jesse replied. He made a decision and put the grenades back into his pocket.

Standing up, Jesse walked down to the trail from the ambush site. He gasped in pain as he bent over and picked up O'Hallohan's weapon, a short-barreled something-or-other. "Look, this trail ends up ahead in about 200 yards. You lead the way, and you can tell me your story. I still have the rifle pointed at your back, so don't trip, or do something stupid." Jesse knew he was starting to run on empty, as an all-encompassing tiredness came creeping up on him.

O'Hallohan told Jesse everything he knew about what had happened to them. The passports and laptops were something Jesse and Leena hadn't known about. Patrick also told Jesse about what the FBI found on the Indiana deputy's email.

So the deputy had been a terrorist after all, Jesse thought.

They arrived at the end of the trail, across the street from the entry road that ran into the church parking lot. It seemed like a century ago that he and Leena had walked down it. They had started up the entry road when a voice behind them shouted, "Stop! Release your guns!"

Jesse didn't know if it was because he was so tired or because they were talking that neither of them had heard the man sneaking up on them.

"I weel not tell you again," the man spat out.

Jesse dropped both guns onto the asphalt with a loud clatter and started to put his hand in his pocket for the grenade.

"Turn around. Which one is Christenson?" When neither answered, the man continued. "It does not matter. I will keel you both."

Jesse opened his mouth, but O'Hallohan stepped forward. "That would be me."

Jesse saw movement to his right. So did the terrorist. There was a flame-like muzzle flash. Bang! Bang! Again and again, over and over. Jesse dropped onto the hard parking lot, hitting his bloody knee. In spite of the pain, he rolled one time, ending up with his rifle and noticing that O'Hallohan had also come up with his own weapon.

The shooter walked over to the terrorist spread out on his back and looked down at him. She kicked out with her right foot, striking the man in the face. "Don't you ever point a gun at my beau," Leena said in a voice that was strained but firm.

"I think he's already dead," Patrick said, getting up and bending over the man to check for a pulse.

"Who's this guy?" Leena asked Jesse.

"Federal agent, Department of Homeland Security," O'Hallohan said.

"I've heard that before," Leena said, squaring off to face O'Hallohan.

"No, don't shoot him!" Jesse yelled. "He's one of the good guys."

"I don't have any bullets left anyway. Why do you think I stopped shooting at that snake?" Leena asked, pointing the gun at the terrorist one more time.

"Nice girl you got there, Mr. Christenson."

"Call me Jesse." He stuck out his hand. "Were you really going to let that asshole shoot you to protect me?"

Patrick shook Jesse's hand. "Not really. I was just trying to get closer to him to make my move."

"An honest cop," Jesse laughed. "Just when I was starting to lose hope."

They heard the sound of sirens then, filling the night air, and could even hear the distant whop of a helicopter approaching.

Jesse suddenly remembered and looked at Leena. "Your mom! I forgot about her."

"It's okay, she's in the church. After the first gunshots the man in the chair ran right past me heading in your direction. By the time I reached the house, mom was standing outside, looking around. I got her into her car and drove back here as fast as I could."

"The gunfire woke her?"

"Yeah. I thought it was just supposed to be a little diversion. What was up with that? It sounded more like the Fourth of July over there."

"One of them was in my house. He tried to shoot me. I shot him with my old shotgun. After that, somebody out front started shooting at me and then there was a sheriff's SUV in my driveway and they started shooting at me. And then another vehicle arrived and they started shooting. I figured it was time to get out of Dodge, so I slipped away. Somehow, our agent friend here caught up with me. Hey, where *did* you come from?"

"The sheriff's SUV crossed the street right in front of us. We were in the second vehicle. As soon as we pulled in, the gang in the front yard and the SUV started shooting at us," O'Hallohan said.

"Us?"

"I head up the Rapid Response Team from Homeland Security, kind of like the civilian counterpart of Delta Force. We were in two Chevy Suburbans. When the bad guys started to shoot, I bailed and made my way over to the creek. I saw one of their men heading down the creek, but couldn't get a shot at him. So I followed and, well, here I am."

"Shouldn't you have a radio or something?" Leena asked.

Even in the dark, you could almost see the color coming to his face. "I, er, have the radio here," he said, pointing to his belt. "But the headset is still on the front seat of the Suburban. We didn't know we were going to end up in the middle of World War III."

"What now?" Leena asked.

"Some of my team probably heard the gunshots just now. If I know them like I think I do, a couple of them will materialize out of that trailhead in just a few minutes. If they haven't already surrounded us."

"Right, Cap," a deep voice called out from the shadows.

Turning in the direction of the voice, O'Hallohan asked, "How many?"

"Counting the one you left on the trail and this one in the drive, six."

"Two complete cells, then."

"Looks that way, sir. We're continuing to sweep."

"Carry on, then."

"One more thing, Cap, there's some FBI agent looking for you."

"Tell him to come up here to the church."

The shadow agent spoke into his headset and then slipped back into the woods and disappeared.

The three started walking to the church.

"It's just like the FBI to get here late," Patrick said. "I guess that's why they have the word 'investigation' in their name—they always miss the action."

Leena walked to the door and knocked three times.

"Secret code, Double-Oh Seven-and-a-half?" Jesse asked.

"She's eighty-two, for Christ's sake," Leena said and then put one hand over her mouth. She crossed herself with the empty pistol as she realized she was standing at the front door to the church. "Oops."

Malie Delaney opened the door and peered out, her eyes falling on the three of them, and finally coming to rest on Jesse. "I thought you were the quiet sort. You sure have kicked up a ruckus tonight."

He looked down at his shoes, grinning. "Sorry."

"Kaikalina told me those men weren't really painters," Malie said. "I didn't think she chose very good ones."

Leena started to object, but Malie cut in. "Sorry, honey, but I thought you'd picked the cheapest ones you could find."

O'Hallohan started to laugh and soon all three of them were laughing so hard they had tears in their eyes. Malie, hands on her hips, just stood there watching them. Only a warrior could appreciate the ridiculousness of it all.

Jesse went into the restroom to clean the blood off himself. The cuts on his hands and knees were nothing more than deep scratches. But the bullet looked like it had struck right at the rib line. There was no exit hole, so it must have lodged somewhere inside. He hoped it just nicked him. Jesse stuffed a paper towel over the hole and pulled his shirt back over it. He intended to have it looked at later, after they reached their destination.

He went back out and joined O'Hallohan and Leena, and the three of them sat in the pews, talking. They saw headlights through the windows and heard the slamming of doors. Malie went to open the front door, which was still locked. In strode a man wearing a blue FBI jacket. Another man stayed behind at the door. "Are these the ones?" he asked of no one in particular.

"Yup. Patrick O'Hallohan," Patrick said, standing up. "You must be Mike Nowiki."

"You're the one I've been talking to in Washington."

"The very same."

"Have you placed them under arrest yet?"

Leena stood up. "For what? We haven't done anything wrong!"

"You put a deputy sheriff in the hospital," Mike stated.

"That was self-defense. He was going to shoot us," Leena said.

"What about the eight dead bodies in Nebraska? You have anything to do with that?"

"No. The Chinese guy did that. He's a hero!" Leena was hollering now, pissed.

"What about shooting the helicopter down with a-a-a...an RPG or something?"

"Where would we get a rocket?" she yelled back, stabbing her finger at him.

"The same place you got that," Mike said, pointing to the M16 Jesse had lying across his lap.

Jesse stood up and put his hand on Leena's shoulder just as she was about to go off again. "Look, we're in church."

Leena sat down.

"This rifle could belong to O'Hallohan," Jesse said. "But you're right, it isn't his. The Chinese agent gave it to me."

"What Chinese agent?"

"The one in Nebraska," Leena said. "Aren't you paying attention?"

Once again, Jesse placed his hand on her shoulder.

O'Hallohan looked at Mike. "I watched a video of the helicopter earlier tonight. I assume Leena filmed that." O'Hallohan looked at Leena for confirmation. "It shows two men firing AK-47s at her." He glanced again at Leena. "You were very brave to get that video. And if that wasn't self-defense, Mike, I don't know what is."

"And tonight?" Mike asked, determined to find a problem.

"I shot one guy. He was in my home shooting at me," Jesse said.

"You guys can't just walk," Agent Nowiki said.

"If you'd been paying attention you'd know that this is all about that car sitting in the parking lot," Leena said, still seething.

"Yeah? So?"

"We've got to be in San Francisco tomorrow," Jesse said. The stress of the past week and the bullet wound were starting to weigh heavily on him. "After that, I'll gladly put myself at your disposal and answer any questions you have. I'll tell you the whole truth. I'm not a liar or thief, ask Him." He pointed up to the statue of Jesus on the cross. "If you want to arrest me then, fine."

"Wait a minute, Jesse. This is bullshit," Leena said, standing up and pointing her finger at Nowiki. "The terrorists have spies in… how many different agencies? I'll call my boss and he can get this, and the helicopter video, on the network under Breaking News five minutes from now."

"She's holding a pretty good hand," Patrick said.

"We can't let you two…" Nowiki paused, seeing Leena raise her eyebrows, "or that car out of our sight again. No offense, but you're a traveling morgue."

"What about letting Agent O'Hallohan accompany us?" Jesse asked, stifling a yawn. "I trust him."

"Deals, deals, always making crappy deals. What happened to the old days when we just threw everybody in jail?" Mike looked over at O'Hallohan. "What do you think? Will your boss go for it?"

"Only one way to find out," said Patrick. He began walking to the office in the back of the church, Nowiki in tow.

"Listen, since you two are here to protect my a—" Jesse stopped, mindful of being in church. "Uh...rear end, I'm going to get a little sleep. I've only had about twelve hours in the last four days."

Leena came over, gave him a kiss on the cheek, and walked back to the office to join the two agents.

Jesse took out the grenades and placed them on the pew before he lay back and curled up with the M16 automatic rifle. He made sure the safety was on, slipped his finger inside the trigger guard, and placed it lightly on the trigger.

Day Five

Chapter 22

The Soldier Returns

Leena touched Jesse's shoulder. "Time to wake up, Sleeping Beauty." She moved her hand over to his face and ran it over the stubble of his beard. "Make that Mr. Scruffy Sleeping Beauty."

"What time is it?" he asked, looking up at the arched ceiling above them.

"About eight. Here, I'll take that." She took the M16 from his hands. "Everybody here was afraid to get it. They thought you might shoot them." She handed the rifle to a large man standing behind her. He pulled the clip out, ejected the unspent round into his hand, and smiled down at both of them before he turned and walked up the church aisle.

Jesse noticed the grenades had also disappeared. "You look great this morning." He ran his fingers through his snarled hair.

"There's a shower in the women's bathroom. I have your bag back there."

"My back is so stiff." He sat up, stretched, and winced. "Where is everybody? It looks like we're alone."

She gave a little laugh. "Wait until you look outside. It looks like a circus."

"Show me this shower first. You smell great. I don't suppose you could find me a cuppa joe."

She smiled sweetly and handed him the cup she'd already placed on the pew in front of him. "You're full of compliments this morning. Remember, you're still in church."

"You truly are a princess." He took a sip of the steaming liquid. "God as my witness, I love coffee."

"I know. Big day today. You better get moving."

The hot water was falling on him when he realized he'd slept better on that church pew than he had in the previous thirty-seven years. When he was suddenly ripped out of Vietnam, there hadn't been any time to come to grips with what had happened there. All these years, he'd carried a tremendous amount of guilt and shame.

Last night in the dark it had all come home to him. All of them, including the enemy, had made poor choices and bad decisions. He was, and had been, an honorable warrior doing his best to fight for that one forgotten man being held down against his will. Every person on earth has a right to live a free life. There is no holier calling than to try to set men free. He had made a stand for freedom.

He stood under the hot water a long time after he finished washing, letting much of the last thirty-seven years run down into the drain, along with the water.

His left knee was sliced open worse than he'd thought from the glass in the house and his dive onto the asphalt. It started bleeding again when he tried to pick glass out of it with the tweezers he carried in his shaving kit. The bullet hole in his left side was black and blue, and the entry wound had an angry red tinge to it. It hurt like a mofo, but he'd concluded last night that if he told anyone about it, it would mean a trip to the hospital and the end of the journey. They'd come too far to surrender now. He had some Band-Aids in his shaving kit, but they were too small to cover the hole. After snooping around the bathroom, he found a roll of duct tape in the cabinet under the sink. He folded a paper towel over the bullet hole and taped it shut. He felt like one of those hicks he always read about.

In spite of being shot, he'd been lucky last night. Lucky. What a weird term, he thought. If he'd been really lucky, the bullet would have missed. Almost every step of this journey had been a chess match. So far, the good guys were winning, but it only took one mistake and that could change. The thoughts were still rolling through his mind when he emerged from the restroom, clean and dressed.

"Hello, Jesse. Welcome back home."

"Father Mark. How are you?"

"I've been better, but I'm not complaining," the priest said with his ever-present smile. "The real question is, how are you?" Father Mark looked up and studied Jesse's eyes. "There seems to be a lot of…uh, activity surrounding your return."

"Transformation from one technology to another is sometimes difficult—"

The door to the church opened and bright sunshine spilled in. "Father, forgive me, but when I heard your last name, I thought you were Irish, too, but you don't look Irish. My name is Patrick O'Hallohan."

Leena was just behind Patrick. She went over and stood next to Jesse.

"I do forgive you. it's what I do, you know," Father Mark said with a smile. "But to answer your question, my mother remarried when I was young and I took my stepfather's name, Fitzpatrick."

"Were you born in Mexico then?"

Jesse was beginning to get irritated at O'Hallohan's questions.

Father Mark smiled again. "Everybody assumes that, because of my brown skin. But no, I was born in LA. My mother was already pregnant when she came here from Syria. My real father died there."

"You don't say?" Jesse said, picking up on O'Hallohan's line of questioning. "I never knew that. Do you have any siblings?"

"Just one older brother. In fact, he called me this week and asked if I knew you, after he saw that report on TV. That's the reason I came by. I told that to the other man out by the door. Does the car really work like you say it does?"

"Yes, Father, everything I said on TV was true." Jesse had a feeling he was going to be saying that often. "Maybe you could give the car a blessing or maybe your brother could. He's a priest, too?"

"He's about the furthest thing from a priest." Father Mark laughed. "He works in the DA's office in San Francisco. My brother is a lawyer."

"Excuse me a second," O'Hallohan said, hurrying out.

"Could you really give the car a blessing, Father?" Leena asked softly.

"Certainly. I've done it many times."

Leena took his arm and started walking him toward the door.

After Leena left and the door closed, taking the sunshine with it, Jesse was left in the dark hallway all alone. A nervous, sick feeling slid over him. He looked around for his .22, but it was gone. Probably taken as evidence. The silence of the church, which he'd always found to be soothing, was now deafening. So much had changed in the past couple of weeks since he'd last been here. He walked to the altar, not knowing whether to be thankful for the yoke God had put on him or to see it as a curse, soon to be removed.

Since he no longer had a pistol, he eased down on his painful knees and prayed to God for protection. He looked up at the statue of Jesus on the cross and for the first time really understood what sacrifice was all about. He prayed that God would give him the strength to finish what he'd started thirteen years ago. Or was it the day he was born? When he finished praying, there was no sense of calm. He just knew what had to be done.

Once a soldier, always a soldier—you're never discharged from the army of good and right. It was time to meet his destiny.

Jesse opened the front doors of the church and walked into the brightness. An armed man standing just outside said something into his sleeve.

"Are you here for me?" Jesse asked.

"Yes, sir, you don't see me. I'm your shadow. But the Cap said you need to put this on," the soldier said, alert eyes looking seemingly in every direction as he held out the vest.

"It's a lot thinner and lighter than the older models."

"It's the latest edition. Kevlar, carbon fiber, and ceramic. It's real light and will stop any pistol shot, but it's not as good with rifle bullets."

Patrick O'Hallohan came out of a large motor home, the command post. "Good. You're dressed."

"Suited up, more like."

"Where's Leena?" O'Hallohan asked and then, spotting her, continued. "I can't keep my men away from her." Jesse glanced over at O'Hallohan. "No, not because she's so beautiful. All my men have been to Iraq and Afghanistan many times. They've seen a lot of news people out in the field. Most of them duck and hide when the action starts and send their camera operators out for the pictures. Last night, Leena put nine out of ten rounds in a two-inch pattern directly into a terrorist's heart. When we told her, she said we counted wrong; there was no way she missed one shot. Christ Almighty, the men love her."

"I know the feeling," Jesse said, a warm glow passing through him.

"You hungry?"

"Starved."

"We've all been going over to eat at the Meadows Restaurant at the golf course. I suppose you already know it's the only place in town for breakfast."

"Yeah, good food." Jesse looked at his Take-Us car. Someone had moved it since last night. "Hey, it's red again."

"Leena and some of my men drove it down to the car wash and blew the other paint off. Leena told me how you did it. Ingenious. When I told my boss how it was accomplished, he said we'd be putting that trick into our manual."

They drove the short mile downhill to the restaurant, located in a small, serene valley with a large meadow that encompassed an eighteen-hole golf course. Tall ponderosa pine and red cedar trees surrounded the entire area.

Later, still at a table in the restaurant, Jesse said, "I don't understand why I have to sign that." He pointed to a thick stack of papers.

"Simply put, we can't guarantee your safety," said the busy little man with the horn-rimmed glasses. He went by the appropriate name of Archibald Goode.

"Once again, I'm not asking you to," Jesse said.

"Like it or not, you became our problem the minute we started protecting you."

"Patrick, can't you do something?"

"My hands are tied. If you don't sign those, we take you into protective custody and stash you somewhere," O'Hallohan answered. "Look, it's just a bunch of legal mumbo-jumbo that says if you get killed, the federal government isn't liable."

"You just hate structure and rules, don't you?" Leena asked.

"That's not true...fully. Give me a damned pen, Archie, but I warn you my lawyer might not like it."

"You don't have a lawyer," Leena said. "Oh, wait! Do you mean Bradford Givings?"

"You, too, Ms. Delaney," Goode said, handing her a set of papers.

"But I'm a journalist! Okay, okay, whatever," Leena said, seeing the look on the man's face. "Quit smiling," she said, trying to ignore the smirk on Jesse's face.

Archibald Goode left. Jesse had finished eating his breakfast, and was enjoying his third cup of coffee.

"You know there is no way to totally protect you," O'Hallohan said. "They could set off an IED anywhere along the route. Someone with an RPG could step out of anywhere. It's the same problem we have in Iraq."

"Leena and I have already discussed that." Jesse put his empty coffee cup down. "If we don't try, they're going to win. There are thousands of people—and who knows, maybe millions of viewers— that expect us to be in San Francisco today. They have no idea of the risk involved. They just want the yoke lifted. We have to get there...or die trying."

"Leena told me about your real plan," O'Hallohan said, glancing at her and then looking Jesse in the eyes. "There will be many people in Golden Gate Park waiting for you."

"Won't they be surprised," he said.

"Lots of good people will be there."

"Yeah and probably a couple of bad guys, too," Jesse pushed his chair away from the table. "I care about those good people, but there's always a price to pay. Too bad. I'm cashed out, let's go."

"Is he always this fatalistic?" Patrick asked Leena.

"Not usually. He's normally optimistic to a fault," she said, her brow furrowed.

"Let's just talk about him like he's not here," Jesse said. "Listen, I know evil. And it always loses. It has to…because evil always turns on itself in the end. It eats itself. It can't help it, that's the nature of it. I just want to make sure we're still alive and well when it happens. Isn't that your job now?" He looked at O'Hallohan, then stood up and pulled out Leena's chair. "It's time to get on with it."

The four-hour drive to San Francisco started at about ten in the morning, when they set out from the church with a Suburban in front and one following. Each vehicle held four well-armed and fierce-looking men. They were all dressed in various outfits, some wearing jeans, some sweats. None of the men had any kind of uniform on.

O'Hallohan begged like a teenager to drive the Take-Us automobile. Jesse had to let him, especially after Leena said the two of them could make out in the back seat. They also had Jesse's bodyguard from the church, riding shotgun.

Leena touched the guard on the shoulder and asked his name. "They call me 'Eyes,'" he replied.

"I, like the letter I? That's a weird nickname."

"I see everything."

"Oh, eyes, like in your head."

"Yeah. Eyes. My eyes never stop moving. I think it's a birth defect. Drives most people crazy, especially the girls I used to date. They always thought I was checking out other girls."

"Well, were you?" Leena asked.

"What?"

"Checking out other girls?"

"Yeah. I couldn't help it." All three burst out laughing.

"It's not my fault. Really."

This made them laugh even harder. It set the mood as they started driving down the mountain.

Jesse realized he wasn't driving and concentrating on the road as he normally would. With Leena at his side, it seemed like the beauty outside the car was more spectacular than ever. The county he lived in was unusual in that the elevation went from about 100 feet above sea level to over 10,000. The seasons moved up and down the mountains at a different pace. It was early spring on the top, and the leaves were just starting to fill out the trees. It was late spring at his house and very green. Summer had already arrived in the valley flatlands, which were turning a golden brown.

The plan, as they were heading down into the foothills, was to stay on Highway 88 until they arrived at Interstate 5 North and then get back on Interstate 80 once again. They had to cross the interior valley to get to San Francisco Bay. Jesse knew a short cut and told them so they would not have to drive through Stockton or Sacramento. The agents were anxious to avoid any city as long as they could. Of course, IEDs could be placed or planted anywhere.

Leena brought up the lack of a police escort.

"We want to keep as low a profile as we can," O'Hallohan said.

Which probably meant they didn't trust any of the local cops, she thought.

When the Take-Us reached Interstate 5, they pulled off the road and switched positions. Jesse was driving once again and the two agents sat in the back seat, each with machine pistols that looked like Uzis.

They were making good time and just getting onto Interstate 80 when Patrick began talking into the microphone in his left sleeve that complemented the earphone in his left ear.

"Good news, bad news," O'Hallohan said. "That was Mike. SF police just had a shoot out with two more terrorists. One was a San Francisco police officer. They don't know who the other is. They're both dead."

"I thought they were operating in three-man cells," Leena said.

"That's the bad news. At least one is still on the loose. Maybe even more cells."

"How many terrorists so far?" Jesse asked. "One in Indiana…"

"Six in Nebraska," Leena said.

"Six last night. That's thirteen," Patrick said.

"And three in the helicopter, and you just said two in the city," Leena added.

"That's eighteen, total," Patrick finished.

"Nineteen would be the same number as the terrorists involved with 9/11, wouldn't it?" Jesse commented. "That would be a fitting end to those bastards." There was something not quite right about the number, but he couldn't put his finger on it.

"Nineteen. Yeah, but we got to find him before he finds us," O'Hallohan said, a chill in his voice.

Chapter 23

The Evil Scent

It was midnight in Tehran. Colonel Mafsanjani jerked back the heavy, dark drapes and stared out his office window. The reflection from his lighter glared back at him from the window as he lit a cigarette. Minutes ago, he'd received an instant message from one of his sleeper agents in San Francisco.

The message said: I went to pick up some additional ordnance for the forthcoming mission. Before I got back to the apartment, the other two members of my unit were assaulted by an American SWAT team. It was a lucky break I wasn't there."

Lucky, the colonel wondered? Or was this sleeper a traitor?

The sleeper agent wanted to know his orders. "Should I continue the mission alone?"

"Of course. Stop the car. Kill them. Kill them all."

This mission was beginning to be very costly, the colonel mused, running his hand through his thinning black hair. He was now missing eighteen of his most trusted agents, all deep cover and very valuable. It would take a decade to replace them. Maybe he should have tried something else, but what else was there to try? He was jarred back to reality by the sound of his phone.

He jammed the phone to his ear. "Speak."

"Colonel, this is Lieutenant Kourani. Sir, we have an American prisoner down here with some unbelievable information. It goes right to the top. I thought you would want to hear it for yourself."

Mafsanjani thought about it: America, the Great Satan. It was they who were backing the Shah's secret police, the very ones who had murdered his pregnant wife. He reached out and once again straightened his wife's picture. "Yes, I'll be right down."

He stubbed the cigarette out and took a last drink, finishing his bitter, cold coffee. Going down to the lowest level always cheered him up.

The elevator doors opened on the ground level. Mafsanjani stepped out of the main elevator, walked briskly across the hall, and inserted his key into the special elevator. He stepped in and wondered briefly at the number of extra guards on duty in the lobby.

When the elevator doors opened on the lowest level, there were two guards standing on either side of the entrance. Mafsanjani stepped out of the elevator and the doors closed behind him. Lieutenant Kourani, wearing a uniform with captain's insignia, stepped out of one of the side rooms, holding an AK-47 and pointing it directly at Mafsanjani.

"Do not move, Colonel," the newly promoted captain ordered. The guards on either side of him held Mafsanjani's arms as the captain came forward and took the pistol out of Mafsanjani's holster.

"You will never get away with this treason," Mafsanjani said, spittle spraying out of his mouth.

"I think he will," said a calm voice. President Ahmadinejad stepped into the hall, accompanied by four men. All had pistols in their hands, aimed at the colonel.

"Your Excellency, what is the meaning of this?" the colonel asked, the first sound of doubt creeping into his voice.

"So it's 'Your Excellency' now, not 'the rabid little nib' anymore?"

"He was the one who said those terrible things," the colonel said, pointing at Kourani. "I have been keeping him under surveillance. He is associating with known enemies."

"Like you, Colonel."

"He is a liar, I tell you! I am no enemy!"

"The captain has told me you've been careless," the president said. "How many agents have you lost this week? What, Colonel? I didn't hear your answer."

"It has been a difficult week."

"You have failed in your duties, have you not? The Take-Us car has not been stopped."

"There is still a chance."

"No, it is too late. Even if you were to succeed now, too many know."

"I beg you, sir, I have always been loyal! My wife died for our cause," the colonel pleaded, doing his best to sound humble. "Give me one more chance."

"I don't think so," the president said. "The only one you've ever been loyal to is yourself."

"I have friends. Think of the mullahs," the colonel said, pulling out his ace in the hole.

"Who do you think sent me?" the president asked, turning to the guards. "Take off his clothes."

"Nooooooo!" the colonel screamed, beginning a fierce struggle.

Two of the president's bodyguards brought it to a sudden halt by shooting their prisoner with taser electrical darts. Mafsanjani flopped on the hard concrete like a dog hit by a speeding car. The men quickly stripped him and dragged him into a small room. The stench of death permeated its walls.

"Fasten him face down," the president ordered.

"No! Allah, I beg you, save me please!" the colonel cried out, tears streaming down his cheeks.

"Beg of Allah all you want. In a minute, he will never even know you existed." The president put on a gown, rubber surgical gloves, and a physician's surgical mask. "You see this, Colonel?" he asked as one of his men, also wearing gloves, held a jar in front of Mafsanjani's face. "This is called lawd."

"Lard, Your Excellency," said the man holding the jar.

"It is pig grease!" the president shouted. He shoved a foot-long metal probe with an electrical wire attached into the jar and swished it around.

"No, no, not that. Allah won't let me in!" The colonel screamed, nearly out of his mind with fear.

The president moved closer, and the colonel could feel the pressure against his backside. The president shoved the electric probe into Mafsanjani's anus. Despite being lubed, it ripped and tore its way into the very center of the colonel. Mafsanjani screamed loud enough for Allah to hear.

"I am told that the pain is nothing compared to what you will feel just a few minutes from now." The president took off the gown, gloves, and mask. "Use all the tools, including wires on his nipples. Those were always his favorite for his other guests. Take your time and make it last as long as possible. Send me the video when you have finished with him, Captain."

"Yes, Your Honorable President," Kourani answered.

After the president left, Kourani bent down and whispered into Mafsanjani's ear before turning on the camera. "You were going to kill me for something my cousin did 8,000 miles away. My American friend said to tell you to rot in hell."

"How could you? I was teaching you all that I know. To follow in my footprints," Mafsanjani whimpered, his breathing strained.

"Oh, but I am." The captain turned the knob ever so slowly to the right.

The colonel's screams tore through the night.

Chapter 24

The Long Sigh

They crossed the Bay Bridge into San Francisco. Jesse had taken the fast lane all the way, with one of the Suburbans directly behind him. Whenever possible, the other Suburban was next to them on the right, effectively shielding the Take-Us from other traffic. O'Hallohan continued cautioning him against following too close to the car in front of them. According to him, this was the safest place to drive. With the thousands of other cars on the road, Jesse thought it was just wishful thinking. They'd turned onto the off ramp, finally saying goodbye to Interstate 80.

They were in San Francisco, almost at the end of the journey.

Leena was on her cell phone, alerting the camera crew that was standing by. The network thought it would be great to do a breaking news update when they pulled up. Three blocks away, the traffic started stacking up. One of the Suburbans was ahead of them and the other was jammed up a couple of blocks behind.

"Better let us out here," Patrick suggested. "Wouldn't be a good thing for us to be caught on camera."

"We'll see you there," Jesse said as O'Hallohan and Eyes got out and started walking down the sidewalk to their final destination.

Leena put her phone down and repositioned the rearview mirror so she could put the small earpiece in. She checked her hair one last time and put the mirror back in place. "Did that bug you?" she asked.

"Nope. Not even a little bit," Jesse lied.

"What did I tell you about lying to me?" she asked, wiggling her finger at him.

"You gonna beat me up right here?"

"Maybe I'll just break your arm." She grabbed his arm, brought it to her mouth, and bit him.

"Ouch! I'm driving," he said, laughing, which made the bullet wound hurt. He continued faking it.

"It's about time you started to smile. We're going to be live in about two minutes." Leena let go of his arm. "Put that big, beautiful smile on. Don't you understand? We made it."

She was right. He did need to lighten up a bit. In front of them and to their left was the camera crew. The camera was trained on the Take-Us and had begun filming. A police officer stopped traffic, and Jesse drove so that the driver's door was next to the curb, with the car facing the oncoming traffic. He slowed down and stopped the Take-Us in the parking spot reserved for them. For the first time in his life, he felt like a conquering hero. They had arrived in front of the book store, their final destination. Boxes of books were stacked one upon another, forming a pyramid. Three men stood behind the stack. Two of them he knew, but not the third.

Jesse opened the door on his side and got out. Leena slid out behind him. A man with a WCN logo on his shirt walked up and handed her a microphone.

"This is Leena Delaney." Excitement and pride swelled her voice. "As you can see, we've just arrived after five days 'On the Road' from New York City to San Francisco in the super-duper, fabulous Take-Us auto. We traveled more than three thousand miles without stopping for gas one time. Since I rode the entire way, I can testify that the automobile, the Take-Us, had not one mechanical problem. Jesse, you've been telling the people all about this dynamic new auto for many days now. Any last words?"

"Most of the people we saw along the way asked the same question: Is this really true? Everything that I've said during these interviews is true," Jesse said, looking directly into the camera. "There will be much pressure to kill this idea, perhaps even me. That's why I met with a publisher in the beginning, even before I began this cross-country excursion."

Jesse walked toward the three men and the boxes of books. One box had been sliced open. He pulled out a book and held it up to show the cover: *The Take-Us,* with a lightning bolt between the Take, and the Us. "There are thousands and thousands of copies of this book being put out on bookshelves all over the country. Each has a special seventeen-digit registration number at the back of the book. You can go to the website and enter that number to receive a VIN number, schematics, and a license from me to build your own Take-Us car. I am allowing just one car per person. This idea, just like the Take-Us car, will create its own energy. With all the thousands of new owners, no one will be able to shut down, buy out, or destroy this concept."

"In case any of you think this is just a publicity stunt," Leena said, taking the microphone, "there is someone here who would like to say something: the Governor of California."

"Yes, thank you." The governor took Jesse's hand in a strong grip. "Mr. Christenson, on behalf of the people of this great state, I would like to give you our thanks. I, like many, have been watching your adventure," he said with that particular gleam in his eyes which had made him famous. "This automobile of yours has the ability to change life in California for the better. Shortly, at my request, a coalition of thirty legislative partners will be introducing a bill into the assembly to make autos like the Take-Us mandatory. Five years from now, there will be no new gasoline-powered automobiles sold in California!"

* * *

At the time the Take-Us stopped at the curb, O'Hallohan and Eyes were waiting at a traffic signal two blocks away. They each wore jackets to conceal their body armor and the weapons they were carrying.

It was a warm day for San Francisco, mid-seventies, and most people on the street were wearing short-sleeved shirts. O'Hallohan thought he and Eyes stood out like two penguins at the beach, but just shook his head. What else could they do? He couldn't hide a machine pistol under a T-shirt.

"Hey, Cap, check it out," Eyes said, tensely.

"Where?"

"Across the street. The priest."

The priest was walking in the crosswalk, directly across from Eyes and Patrick. He was headed in the direction of the interview. "Yeah, what about him?"

"He's not wearing a cross."

"Under his coat?"

"Why does he have a coat on? And he's dark, like a Mexican or an Arab."

"Lots of both in California," O'Hallohan said, trying to see more clearly.

"He has on a long coat, and his hands are in the pockets."

"Maybe he's cold."

"Sir, look closely. He's sweating."

"Like Baghdad. Holy shit."

The light turned green and they moved. "Go down this side, Eyes. Try to get in front of him." Damn, O'Hallohan thought. He spoke quietly into his left sleeve.

When the priest turned right, O'Hallohan saw his face, and with mild shock, recognized Father Mark's brother, the lawyer. He was walking at a determined, moderate pace down the sidewalk. O'Hallohan had no choice. He crossed the busy street and dodged through the oncoming traffic, making it to the other side. No one even honked at him during the dangerous stunt.

O'Hallohan saw Eyes on the other side of the street. He had run down the sidewalk and was already at the next light. Eyes stopped, looked, and ran through the intersection. Then he crossed over to the same side of the street that the priest was on. The two agents now had the priest sandwiched. If the priest noticed anything strange about the running man, he didn't show it.

O'Hallohan advanced until he was just a few steps behind the priest and could see the unusual bulge under the coat the man wore. The priest's right hand was stuffed deep in his pocket. His left arm was out and next to his side, that hand empty.

They had come to the crosswalk, and O'Hallohan spoke again into his sleeve. His jacket was already unzipped. When the light turned green, he turned his back to the priest, allowing the man to walk into the intersection. O'Hallohan put out his arms. The surrounding pedestrians stopped when they saw the machine pistol strapped to his chest. He showed his badge with his left hand and put a finger to his lips with his right. Please let no one complain for the next few seconds, he prayed.

Eyes had his back to the priest on the other corner, and whatever he was doing had all the people on that corner moving backward.

O'Hallohan dropped his badge and pulled his gun free. He spun around to the priest.

The woman on his right screamed.

The priest hesitated and then stopped in the middle of the street, slowly turning around.

"You! Priest! Get down on the ground!" O'Hallohan shouted. "Everybody down!" O'Hallohan dropped to the sidewalk as the pedestrians scrambled to get away.

Across the street Eyes had his weapon trained on the fake priest's back. The man looked directly at O'Hallohan and started to raise both arms. There was a wire trailing from his right hand back into his pocket. "Allahu Ak—"

Both agents' guns boomed at the same moment. The terrorist collapsed and sprawled on the asphalt, his head a bloody pulp.

A black Suburban squealed around the corner and stopped over the body of the terrorist lying in the street. The driver's door flew open and an agent jumped out and sprinted away from the vehicle. He was twenty feet away when the dead terrorist, in his last act, relaxed his finger off the trigger button.

Even a block away, the explosion was ferocious. The concussion shattered windows all around them. Jesse could see the SUV still in the air as he stared toward the scene. It seemed to hang there for a second before it came crashing down. When the blast stopped rever-berating, there was a moment when time seemed to stand still, and quiet reigned. Then, like a dam bursting, there was chaos. Around him, everybody was in motion.

The governor's bodyguards hustled him to a waiting limo. The news crew leaped up and ran toward the blast, Leena in the lead. The four agents guarding Jesse and Leena had finally arrived and now split up, two of them running next to Leena, trying to talk her into staying back, out of whatever danger might be coming next.

"Good luck with that," Jesse said softly under his breath.

"Do you always come into town with such a bang?" Bradford F. Givings asked.

"Good God, Brad. How many did I kill this time?"

"You didn't kill anyone. It's simply in motion now. Change is always painful."

"Last week hardly anyone knew I existed. Now half the world hates me."

"Well, that just means you now have the qualifications to run for president," Givings said, smoothing an invisible wrinkle in his expensive suit.

"Like anyone would vote for me." Jesse watched the hubbub unfolding down the street.

"By next year, your name will be more familiar than any other name in the country."

"Yeah, right. How did you get the governor to show up?" Jesse asked as the limousine tore away, tires squealing.

"Easy. He never met a camera he didn't like."

The scream of sirens filled the air. There were many of them... too late again, of course.

"You could be the next governor."

"You're serious. I think you've been smoking something."

They stared down the street at the scene of the explosion. Leena was walking back toward them, Patrick O'Hallohan holding her arm. Her hands were flailing. There was blood on the front of the O'Hallohan's pants.

"She's a fiery little thing, isn't she?" the lawyer commented.

"I think fierce is more correct."

Leena and O'Hallohan got to the front of the bookstore.

"What happened?" Jesse asked.

"Suicide bomber," O'Hallohan said. "I'll tell you about it after I get you both off the street."

"Brad, I want you to look at the letter I signed about all this protection. It can't be legal," Leena said.

"Mr. Christenson, Jesse…" O'Hallohan said, an exasperated look on his face.

"Come on, sweetheart, let's go inside. We didn't come this far to be killed on the sidewalk." Jesse turned to Givings. "Fiery might have been the correct word, after all."

"Brad doesn't know anything," Leena said. "He's an asshole."

"Did I miss something about your trip?" Wincing, the lawyer opened the door to the bookstore.

They went inside, and the manager led them to his office. Then he went back outside to watch the excitement. They couldn't leave the building even if they wanted to. The streets were blocked with emergency vehicles, and more were continuing to arrive.

The four took seats at a polished oak conference table. Jesse once again asked what happened down the street.

O'Hallohan sighed. "Eyes spotted a phony priest and we tried to get him to surrender. When I was in Iraq, we were trained to spot suicide bombers. These are cold-blooded killers, not innocent, sacrificial lambs. When they start to raise their hands toward heaven—the sky—they always say 'Allahu Akbar.' God is greater. After they take their hands out of their pockets, it's normally too late, because the trigger is built so that once they hold down the button the bomb is activated. When they release the button, the bomb explodes. So, when you shoot someone like that, they involuntarily clench their fingers into a fist, activating the bomb. Then when death sets in, all their muscles relax and they release the button, exploding the bomb. Eyes and I both shot him."

"And then, boom. Goodbye terrorist number nineteen," Jesse

said, slashing his fingers across his throat. "I'm happy we got him, but—oh my god, what about civilian casualties?

"One of my men saw what was going down and drove the Suburban over the body, then got out and ran. That was quick thinking. The armored SUV took the brunt of the blast. That agent saved a bunch of lives—I'm going to recommend him for a medal. He got some shrapnel in the legs. The murderer had the bomb packed with roofing nails; I already pulled one out my thigh. I hope he didn't coat them with rat poison like they do over there."

"Rat poison? Why would they do that?" Givings asked.

"Oh, come on, Brad. Don't you ever watch our news reports?" Leena asked. Jesse saw her mouth the word "asshole" under her breath.

"It keeps the blood from clotting. More people die that way," O'Hallohan said. "They bleed to death. Now that I think of it, I'm going to see a paramedic."

Federal Agent O'Hallohan limped out of the room.

"He doesn't even realize he's a hero," Leena said.

Chapter 25

The Promise Fulfilled

Jesse glanced at Leena and then at the lawyer, who had his briefcase open and was digging for something.

"Please tell me you don't have a gun in there," Jesse said without a smile on his tired face.

Givings looked up and smiled. "A pistol would equate to a spit wad compared to this." He plopped a thick packet of papers onto the oak table. "GM was willing to match the Iranian's offer of a hundred million dollars…cash."

"I told you that wasn't going to be acceptable."

"That's what I told them."

"And?"

"They agreed. You got what you wanted. They were shocked you didn't ask for more money up front."

"I didn't want *any* money up front."

"I thought you'd say that, but General Motors wanted to make sure we didn't change our minds later, so they legally locked us into a contract. Great for us. Besides, since when is one of the world's largest corporations going to miss a few million bucks? You'll need some money up front to pay your legal expenses." He reached for his gold pen. "That's me and my office, you know."

"Yeah, whatever," Leena said, getting up and standing behind Jesse. "Didn't I give you that pen for your birthday?" she asked Givings while rubbing Jesse's neck.

"What about the name?" Jesse asked, changing the subject.

"No problem. It'll be 'Take-Us,' designed in a minimum height of two inches, in gold, with a lightning bolt between the two words. They'll use it on all the cars they build."

Good, Jesse thought, and wondered if somewhere up in heaven his Kristin was smiling down on him. "How are they going to structure the payments?"

"They couldn't believe you only wanted two percent for a licensing fee."

"I only wanted one percent." Jesse wiggled his shoulders when Leena started massaging a particularly tight spot.

"I know." Givings tapped the pen twice. "I went in high and they didn't even try to talk me down. Their lawyer told me after the meeting they had previously agreed to go up to twenty percent. Their sales must really be lagging."

"What's it calculated on?"

"As we discussed, it will be the last line on the dealer's invoice, after all the options are subtotaled. The last line will simply say 'Take-Us Licensing Fee,' and it will be two percent of everything above it. That's really ingenious. It doesn't cost the manufacturer anything; the consumer pays it all."

"If all the different manufacturers do the same thing, it will be fair to all, as long as they don't phony up the invoices and try tacking a really large dealer markup fee under it. I just want to be fair."

"I've got all that covered in the contracts. You're going to have to hire a large accounting company to manage the auditing. I'll help with that. You should incorporate—"

"Whoa, whoa. I know I have much to do."

"Listen, Jesse. If you figure there are three hundred million autos in the United States, and within the next ten years they'll all be replaced with a Take-Us type car, and if the average sales price were a conservatively low $25,000, you'd receive $500 on every car sold. You do the math. And that's just in the United States. There's still the rest of the world. In a couple of short years you're going to be one of the richest men in the world."

"Did you know that?" Leena asked, looking around at him. "Let's see, five hundred times three hundred million…Wow!" She dropped into the nearest chair.

"Are you sure?" Jesse didn't move, stunned.

"You really didn't know, did you?" Givings said, looking him in the eye. "The real beauty of it is that it's a total cash business. Your one great idea is going to change the world in a positive way, and you'll be rewarded in the same fashion. It seems you're about to receive your Ph.D. from that school you told me about. Here, sign this." The lawyer tapped the pen and placed it beside the papers.

"What is it?" Jesse asked.

"It's the agreement to agree. Just sign it so GM can give us some money. The real contracts will take weeks to be drawn up."

Jesse signed the papers and firmly laid the pen on the table.

"One more thing. Sign this, appointing me as your legal representative."

"You mean your firm?" Jesse asked.

"No, I mean me. I quit the firm. You are now my first client. That speech you gave me about values and patriotism made me realize what was truly important. You sold me."

"Oh my God, Brad. Be careful. Your heart just doubled in size and might blow," Leena said, getting up and giving him a hug. "Welcome to humanity."

Jesse didn't know what to say, so he stayed silent. It seemed it was never too late to change.

Givings's eyes had a sheen to them as he put the pen in an inside pocket, took the papers, and shoved them back into his briefcase. He glanced at his watch and stood up. "I've got to be going. I'm booked on a flight for Tokyo in a few hours. I've got appointments with Toyota and Honda. I'd be willing to bet big money that by the time I leave Japan, the rest of the car manufacturers will want to make appointments to see me."

"One second, Brad," Leena said.

The lawyer saw the look on her face and sat back down. "What is it?"

"I'm not sure what we're allowed to say, but you need to go to China, too."

"Good God, I almost forgot our promise," Jesse said, picking up on Leena's request. "We had a bit of trouble out on the road. We need to make the Take-Us available in China."

"How much trouble? Look, I'm your lawyer," Brad said.

"I think we'll be okay," Jesse said, "but we had an incident the government wants hushed up. If we need you for any of that we'll let you know, but just see if you can make some kind of initial contact with the Chinese."

"I'll do as you request. However, I want the whole story when I return."

The lawyer left the two of them in the small room in the back of the bookstore.

"We spoke before about unintended consequences," Jesse said. "I swear I never saw this coming."

"What *did* you see coming?" Leena asked in a curiously sexy voice.

"All I ever wanted in my life was someone to love. I had it once, and after it was snuffed away I thought I was doomed to spend the rest of my years alone."

"Someone to love…that's my dream also, my sweet man." She sat on his lap and buried herself ever so softly in his arms.

He once again got lost in her kiss. It seemed that he was always coming up for air. "I believe you, Kaikalina. Now, how about we get out of here?"

"I'm sure we can find a hotel around here. Maybe one with a honeymoon suite," she said, raising her eyebrows. "You must think I'm the horniest person in the world."

"Second horniest," he said, beginning another kiss.

They walked out of the bookstore holding hands. A small crowd was gathered across the street. The crowd recognized the two of them and started hooting and clapping, except for two men who turned their backs and started walking away.

At the curb, a dark-skinned policewoman heard Jesse and Leena approach. She turned to face them. In her hands, she held a ticket book.

"This your car?" she asked, gesturing at the Take-Us. "Are you Jesse Christenson?"

A slow sigh of relief escaped Jesse's lips. "Yes. Are you an Arab?" He couldn't hold back the words; they just tumbled out of his mouth.

"Me? Hell, no. I'm from Mexico. But we don't even park like this down there." She handed Jesse a parking ticket. "Don't you even know which way you're headed? Are you coming or going or what?"

Jesse looked at Leena. She silently mouthed the word "coming," and they both burst out laughing.

He was laughing so hard he bent over. As he stood up straight with tears of delight in his eyes, he felt two bullets strike him in the chest, spinning him around and knocking him off his feet. The back of his head struck the sidewalk, arms splaying out from his sides, feet together.

The acrid stench of the city filled his lungs. Quiet fuzziness surrounded him and a black perimeter started to come to a point around his vision. Jesse could feel blood flowing from his side, and he tasted his own breath. He looked up at the once-clear, blue sky through tear-filled eyes. Then the darkness beckoned him.

His eyes closed.

About the Author

John R. Takacs was born and raised in Mishawaka, Indiana. As one of two boys among seven siblings, he had plenty of babysitters, fellow conspirators, and willing teachers growing up. But it was in the library that he developed his lifelong habit of reading. Following high school graduation, Takacs enlisted in the United States Army. He served with the famed 101st Airborne Division in Vietnam, where his helicopter was shot down by mortar fire. Takacs sustained serious injuries and was awarded the Purple Heart Medal. After an honorable discharge, he attended Indiana University.

Takacs landed a job as a high-rise ironworker, where he cultivated the need for an adrenaline high that his Army career had fostered. He also enjoyed tinkering, inventing a number of time-saving devices, and went on to own several small businesses.

After retiring and writing his first book, Takacs found he had become overweight and sedentary. Determined to make a change, he resolved to drop the extra weight and get back to the activities he enjoyed as a younger man. His nonfiction book, *Doing a 180 at 60*, details this journey, which started at the age of sixty. He enjoys racing motorcycles, skydiving, skiing, scuba diving, bicycling, and mountain climbing. As a leading proponent of active lifestyle, he hosts "Doing a 180 at 60" on KVGC Radio.

Takacs is currently working on the sequel to *Hidden Truths*, which is an updated version of his award-winning book, *The Take-Us*. The sequel, *Sealed Truths*, continues Christenson's quest to free America from dependence on OPEC and Big Oil.

Takacs, along with his wife Monika, resides in Pioneer, California.

Visit him at www. johnrtakacs.com.

Acknowledgements

My heartfelt thanks and sincere wishes go out to so many of you. I begin with my wife Monika, whose constant belief and love sustained me though so many of life's challenges. In the very early years of my writings Jody Lawlor convinced me that the gift of imagination was my greatest strength as a writer. The Gold Rush Writers group taught me many of the book business basics as well as authors Antoinette May and Dr. Helen Bonner, who showed me the intricacies of the author's life.